Shattered

Shattered

Tom Wilson

Published in 2016 by Wide Margin,
90 Sandyleaze, Gloucester, GL2 0PX, UK
http://www.wide-margin.co.uk/

ISBN 978-1-908860-16-3

Printed and bound in Great Britain by Lightning Source,
Milton Keynes

Teacup

"What the hell is happening to me, Father? What the hell?"

Tears were streaming down John's face. He had a beard that was at least a week old. I had never seen him anything other than clean-shaven before. He looked down at the tiles of his kitchen floor, dark grey with off-white grout. "That were her favourite one, that were."

He pointed to the shattered teacup in the middle of the floor, the delicate porcelain shards scattered in an explosion of grief.

"She loved it," he sobbed. "Never kept it for special. Every day was a special day if you made it so, she always said. And now I've gone and bloody broken it. She'd kill me if she weren't already dead. I don't cry, me, I never do. What the hell is happening to me, Father?"

"Your wife died a week ago John, and I've come to talk to you about her funeral. Do you want me to sweep up the pieces, maybe put them somewhere safe for now?"

"Yeah, I guess. I'll find an ice cream tub. We've got loads. It was all Marion ate for the last few weeks of her life."

I'd been to visit Marion enough times in the past year, so I knew where the dustpan and brush were kept—under the sink, hardly an original place. I got them out and carefully began to sweep the pieces up. Death shatters so much, including crockery. "We used to live in a house with tiles like these," I said as I swept, "By the time we left, it has claimed about twenty cups, glasses, plates and the like. Toddlers and tiled kitchen floors was a lethal combination."

It was a pretty rubbish attempt at cheering John up, and it failed. "Yeah, but Marion was always so careful. Never broke anything in the fifteen years we've lived here. I put them tiles down myself. A mate got them for me, and although they weren't quite the colour she wanted, she said we should have them because they were cheap. Never wasted a penny, did Marion."

John sniffed, wiping his tears into the sleeve of his jumper. "I dunno why I was bothering being posh with you anyway, a mug's more your style isn't it?"

"Yeah, that'd be great thanks. No sugar though, just milk."

John busied himself with the alchemy of tea making, that great calming art of the English. Two mugs—both with YNWA emblazoned on them in red and gold—two tea bags, some milk, two sugars for him. Kettle boiled, pour, stir, squeeze the bag out, add the milk, add the sugar, a simple and calming ritual, which was just what he needed to put his defences back in place.

"Right, let's go talk about church," he said, squaring his shoulders, ready for combat. "Not too much of that religious crap, right Father."

The old John was back, for a moment at least. I liked John. Talking with him was refreshing. All too often, people who think I'm mad for being a vicar treat me with courtesy, respect, friendliness even. But it only ever goes so far, and you have a fairly clear idea after a while that they are being defensive, not letting you get too close in case you try and convert them. Essentially, they think Christians are weird, and while they may tolerate the weird person in their midst, they do not actually want to be friends with them. Ideally they just want to avoid a prolonged conversation, but sometimes needs must. But John just told me he thought I was weird, and once that was established, the barrier to friendship was gone.

"When you say you don't want any 'religious crap,'" I asked, "What exactly did you have in mind for a funeral service held in a church?"

He sighed. Tired, still defeated by the death of his beloved wife of thirty-seven years. Married at nineteen and twenty-one, life-long devotion cut short before the happy retirement they had been planning and dreaming for. Cancer is cruel. Actually, all death is cruel, and right now I am really not sure what to make of it. Since Mum died, I just do not have any certainties any more.

Time was, an encounter with someone like John would have been quite straight forward. I am used to spending time with people in the last few weeks and months of their lives. Watching them grow frailer, listening to the anger, the regrets, the pain. Wishing they had worked less, seen the kids more, said "I love you" more often, all that and more. Trying to assist them in making their peace with their family, friends and God, if they believe in him. Dad's death gave me hope for all of that. He was wonderful at it.

Dad had been not quite right for a few months, but being male, had not wanted to bother the doctor, not till he found taking the dog for a walk was getting to be a struggle. A few weeks of tests later, it turned out he had pancreatic cancer, it was quite advanced and there was no hope of a lasting cure. He refused all forms of chemo, and got to work preparing to die. He summoned his family and friends, and we all came, at our appointed times, for our appointed conversations. I prayed with him, anointed him with oil, gave him communion. It felt like that was the sort of thing I was ordained for. Here was a man prepared to meet his Maker. Seemed kind of old-fashioned in a way, but also kind of wonderful. Of course I was sad when he died, crying secretly in the shower the morning before his funeral, but taking it nonetheless, shoulders squared to lead the coffin into church. This is what I do, of course I'm going to take Dad's funeral. Why wouldn't I?

I'm glad I did, but there was no way I would have taken Mum's. If Dad's death was wonderful, hers was horrific. Dementia is a cruel killer, stealing the mind and leaving the body to waste away, a dribbling, wretched wreck. My mother died fourteen months before her body did, if not even earlier. Over a year of almost daily visits to a wizened old woman who swore and cursed me for stealing her rabbits or hiding her chocolates, it burnt a hole in my soul that I am still waiting to heal.

Marion did begin to heal me. She knew something of the pain I had faced, the whole church did. I did try and hide it at first, but it became too much, and I had to talk about it. I tried to keep it out of the pulpit, but over coffee, in people's houses, I began to give honest answers to those innocuous questions "How are you?" and "How's your mum?"

They're not really questions, are they? "How're you?" normally means "I have acknowledged you are present and since you are upright and look healthy I assume you are fine. Can we get on with the purpose for our meeting?" I try and only ask it as a genuine question, expecting a genuine answer. People in church had to learn to do the same when talking with me. Otherwise they got an answer they were not expecting. "Pretty rubbish, actually. What about you?" is not exactly how you expect the vicar to respond to your polite greeting.

Marion's cancer was a slow burn, gradually eating its way through her life. She did opt for chemo the first time, back when both Mum and Dad were alive. It kept the cancer at bay, gave her a whole new lease of life. With a wig she was confident, outgoing, and ready to face anything. John teased her about the wig, bought her a red one for the football, which she wore quite happily. But six years later, as it often does, the cancer came back. It had retreated, regrouped deep within her body and now it came back for total war. It was devastating. In November she was fine. By January, a wreck.

Yet she faced it all with dignity, even managing to smile and laugh with her visitors. I came once, maybe twice a week. Marion was a pillar of the church, as they say, and when a pillar begins to give way, you go first to shore it up and then to gently lay it down while working all the time to put a different one in place elsewhere. The thing was, Marion said that to me.

Sitting in her living room, her beloved cup and saucer of tea on a little table by her side, she commented to me one grey January morning, "People used to say I was a pillar of the church. Thing is, this pillar's crumbling. You need a new one in its place, Paul. Better get to building. Either that, or you'll have some wreckage to sift through."

I could not think of a reply at first. Then I realised she was giving me an opportunity to be honest. To talk about death as a reality, to not wrap the pain up in the sugar of a metaphor, to take the medicine of impending death with all its bitter aftertaste like a grown man. "I'm really sorry you are dying, Marion. There is nothing I can do to stop that. But I'll happily hold the pillar and ease it to the floor, try and avoid a big crash and clouds of dust making a right mess of the nave."

She smiled back, thanking me for my honesty. "You know, it is so much easier when people use the d-word and admit you're dying. Means we can start from where we are, not from where we wish to be."

Marion was always business-like about the important things. We had a wonderful chat for about an hour, ranging from being sure you had apologised from past faults through thinking of what possessions to leave for which relative and finally what was important in planning a funeral. I wish I had that sort of conversation more often, instead of it being a once in an age, this is why I do this job—for this sort of golden moment. Even with Marion, I only had that conversation once. Maybe she sensed that things were about to go downhill. She had been gently strolling down towards the valley of the shadow of death, and all of a sudden, within a week of that conversation, her body started to stumble headlong to the valley floor. Cancer eats its way through a person, showing no mercy, giving no quarter. It was ravenous and although drugs might sate its hunger for a while, they were never going to be enough.

John knew Marion was dying. She knew he knew. He knew she knew he knew and so on. Her death was something real, something immanent, but still something neither he or I were really truly ready for. I think that she was ready to die by the end. In fact, I think she was ready to die from that conversation in January. It was almost as if she decided she had got her house in order, and that was it, time to go meet her Maker.

It gave me a brief glimmer of hope that the Weasel would not be with me forever, that the cruel bastard dementia, who took my Mum away, was not the final master. That maybe there was some truth in St Paul's oh-so-bloody-annoying comment about the sting of death being taken away. But it was only a glimmer, and then she died, and here I am, standing with John looking at a shattered tea cup, wondering how I pick up the pieces of his messed up life, of my messed up life, of the fact that I am not sure I believe there is anything other than oblivion lurking in the valley of the shadow of death. "You're born, you live, you die, that's it" was how I once heard a student sum it up, back when I was doing mission work in Leeds university. At the time I thought her life so bleak and helpless. Pretty young twenty-year old blond girl, with no ultimate meaning or purpose to her life. I tried to persuade her otherwise, but to no avail. Now I am starting to have a sneaking suspicion that maybe she was right.

Preparing to say goodbye

"Okay, John, so if we're not having too much religious crap, what are we having for the church service then?"

The shards of the teacup were stored in an ice cream tub for now. We were in his living room, filled with cards expressing "Sympathy at your loss," and other such weak and slightly ineffective sentiments. I was doing my best to get back into professional mode. Cup of tea on the table next to me. Notebook out. Example service sheet at the ready. List of questions poised. "Shall I talk you through what will happen?"

The familiar patter of the familiar routine of planning a funeral was kicking in. No need to think and feel the pain too much just for the moment. I know what I am doing here. I know how to do this well. I recently tried to count up the number of times I have had this conversation. Fifteen years in ministry means it must be well over a thousand times by now. Dull the pain with the routine. Focus on John, leave your own scars and scabs for the time being. Plenty of time to pick at them later.

"Yeah, you tell me what will happen." Another sigh. He was not really ready to take control of his life yet, happy to let others guide him for the moment, while the shattered piece of his life swirled just outside of his control in the storm of his grief.

"So, as the coffin comes in to the church, there will be some music playing. You need to decide what—a CD or something on the organ, up to you. Then we have the welcome, a hymn—again, you need to decide what. Then an opportunity for someone from the family to say something if they would like to, but only if they really want to. Then a Bible reading and talk. Then the prayers, a second hymn, a few closing words and then we leave the church, to another piece of music. At the crem it is really quite short, just music to come in to, a few words from me, the curtains close, and we leave to another piece of music."

"Lots of music then? I've got a few ideas. Certainly for the last piece."

"Yeah, quite a lot. What music have you chosen?"

Often a dangerous question. Sometimes the answer is straight forward, sometimes it is really touching, occasionally my mental eyebrows leave my forehead and can only get back down by parachute. This being Liverpool, there are two popular choices for what to play after the curtains close and the blessing has been said. "Zed cars" or "You'll never walk alone." The crem attendant is a staunch Evertonian.

14

"You're in my heart. You're in my soul." I can only guess at the pain to his soul of Gerry and the Pacemakers singing "You'lll neeeeevaah waaaaalk aaaloooone" anything up to ten times a day. It probably just makes him all the more passionate on Derby Day.

John is not really a football fan. That is to say, he only thinks about the match on the day of the match, and has been known to not spend the entire game in front of a telly offering his views on what the Red Men should be doing. More to the point, Marion was not that interested either. She was a Red all her life, but not militant about it, and took the rough with the smooth, just glad that either of the teams from her beloved city were doing well.

So that was the football themes rejected. "Something to dance to, that's what I want," John told me. "She always liked to dance. A bit of the Beatles maybe. I'll have to think."

"Just so long as its not 'Bat out of hell'," I offer, with a wry smile.

"Nah, I hate Meatloaf. And even I think that is a bit poor taste," John reassures me with a shake of his head.

Music communicates so much, if chosen aptly. If it is the first of a couple to die, then their partner will choose a special song, one that captures the romance of their relationship. I think this is what John was thinking of. He and Marion were both fans of the Beatles, and I can imagine them dancing together to many of their hits. The question remained though, which one best summed them up? Fortunately that decision did not have to be made today, although there were plenty of others that did.

"Well, the music for the crem is something you need to tell the funeral directors, not me."

"Oh, I'm seeing him tomorrow, so I'll have a look at my CDs tonight, and pick some. Did you say we can have CDs at the church as well?"

"Yeah, course you can. How about you pick 4 pieces on CD—two for the church, and two for the crem, and then we have two hymns in the service? That'll avoid at least a bit of religious stuff, won't it?"

"Sounds good to me." John nodded his assent and sipped his tea. "As for the Bible reading, you pick it. Marion wrote down her two favourite hymns for me: 'In Christ Alone' first and 'Abide with me' second, she said. Apparently we should all know 'Abide with me,' cos they sing it at the FA Cup final." A hint of a smile.

"It is a good choice, most people will know it. The church folks will know and love 'In Christ alone,' so there should be some good singing. What about someone saying anything? I assume you won't want to, but will anyone else?"

"Nah, we'll leave that to you mate. That's what you're paid for."

With that comment, that little putting me in my place, I realized that John was going to be okay. It would take a long time, of course it would, but healing would come eventually; with a lot of talking, secret crying, and reminiscing, healing would eventually come.

"It would be a genuine honour," I said. I really meant it, as I had loved having Marion in church. Time to get to work on marshalling the details of her life.

"So remind me, when was Marion born?"

For the next fifteen minutes, John retold Marion's life from his perspective. He knew a few details of her early life: date and place of birth, an idea of where she went to school. After the slightly hazy start, he was on to firmer ground when we got to Marion's adult life. He talked confidently of her first job at the Coop, of her second job at the Coop, moving to work in the cafe at lunch times. He talked about going in for his lunch, being struck by how pretty one of the serving girls was, asking her, joking, half-expecting a put-down, if she was free that evening, and being heart racingly excited when she said that actually she would be happy to meet him for a cup of coffee, but "no silly stuff, mind you behave yourself. I'm a good Christian girl."

John was on his best behaviour that night, and many other nights afterwards. He remembered fondly the first time he managed to get his arm around Marion (in the cinema as it happened) and how they started to hold hands when they walked together in public. They were married at St Mark's, and that is "probably the last time I went to a service there. No, tell a lie, I have been to a few funerals recently."

Marion loved the church, got stuck in to life there, taking her girls to the mums and toddlers, then when she was a housewife with girls at school helping out at the lunch club. She went back to work for a while, but still kept coming to St Mark's on a Sunday and a Thursday evening

Bible study. Marion was an armchair Red, an avid reader of murder mystery novels, fond of saying, "It's gonna be all right pet," and "Don't worry love, the good Lord's got it all in hand," and a genuine Beatles fan as well. John mentioned holidays in Spain as well as in Rhyl and Prestatyn when the kids were younger.

By the time he was finished and I had recapped the details, I had two sides of scribbled notes, plenty of threads to weave into a small tapestry of her life.

"Thanks, John." A swig of nearly cold tea, then another gulp to finish it before it got too cold to be palatable.

I paused, hoping he was a comfortable in the silence as I was.

"One more thing: who do you want me to pray for by name?"

"What?" He was confused. My fault.

"Sorry, I should have explained more clearly. One of the prayers in the funeral service includes an opportunity to pray for family members by name. Obviously I'll mention you, but who else?"

"The girls: Elsa is the oldest and Megan the youngest. Their fellas, Steve and Terry as well. And their kids. Umm. Will is the oldest, then, oh which is it, Jack, then Olly."

"Right, so John, Elsa and Steve, Megan and Terry, Will, Jack and Olly. That sound okay to you?"

"Yeah, fine."

"Thanks, John." I could see he was tired now. "Shall we leave it there for now? I'll go and write all this up, then come round tomorrow afternoon with a draft order of service and that for you to see."

"Okay. I think you sometimes print them at the church don't you?"

That probably meant John wanted to spend as little as possible. We do print orders of service at church, for no charge. It takes me about fifteen minutes to do them normally, and the printing cost is always less than a fiver, as we just do black-and-white copies on white paper. The cheap option for those who cannot—or do not want to—spend much on a funeral.

"Yeah, I can do that. Do you have a photo you want me to use for the front cover? There's some nice ones up on the mantlepiece."

We both stretched and stood in front of the black mantlepiece, either side of the gas fire. We discussed the photos together, settling on one of Marion at the seaside, somewhere in Spain John thought, but no idea which resort. The bright blue sky, her smiling face, she did not look like she had a care in the world.

"Who'd've thought. That was only last summer."

"It's a lovely photo mate, a real good choice. I'll take it with me, and bring it back round tomorrow. Three o'clock okay?" I asked, getting out my phone and opening my diary app.

"Yeah, fine. The funeral guy is coming at 11, so I'll tell him you'll sort the service sheet. Do I have to pay you?"

"No, it's all done by them. The fee is included in what they charge you. And you're not paying me, you're paying the church." I always feel slightly guilty about the money. I mean, I am doing a professional job, and professionals deserve to be paid, but there is something slightly uncomfortable about making money from other people's tragedies. Still, I can console myself that Anglicans are normally cheaper than civil celebrants, and do a better job in my completely biased opinion.

We shook hands, and I patted John on the shoulder with my other hand as we shook. I do not know him well enough to give him a real hug, yet. His eyes glistened as another flood of grief prepared to wash out of him. He blinked the tears away.

Time to go, I thought. Let the man cry in peace.

"See you tomorrow, John. God bless."

"See you Father."

Imagine

When it is a wet, cold February evening and you just want to go home, you stand around for ages until eventually your bus comes as part of a pack, two or three leapfrogging each other past the stops. Funerals seem to sometimes do that as well, jostling for your attention and time, although if I lift my gaze from my navel for a moment, I have to recognize that this is not really a big problem. I hate funerals, but my pain is probably not the agony I am claiming it is.

The next morning, I had two separate phone calls from funeral directors, both requesting crem-only funerals the following Friday. Fortunately there was a breathing space. 10:30 and 11:30 slots meant I would have half an hour to draw breath and rearrange my notes. And happily the first was a man, 79 year old Harold Griffiths and the second a woman, 73 year old Linda Groves. I once had to do the funerals of two Sheilas on the same day. It still makes my heart race a little bit to think back to it. I checked my notes so many times I was nearly word perfect with the eulogies, and even double checked with the family of the first Sheila,

Sheila Jones I think it was, as I retold the story of her life that they had told me.

Death is so instant, so quick and yet so final, so everlasting. In my younger days I never thought I was actually immortal, but I never really thought about death. As a kid I never saw anything related to death really. Actually, that is not true. Cartoons are full of things that ought to lead to the deaths of minor characters, and the chase scene of any decent action film leaves a trail of bodies, except we never stop to think that all those car crashes must have resulted in fatalities. I certainly never did.

But now I think about them all the time. Takes the fun out of many films, if watching death and destruction could ever have been described as actually being fun. Maybe that's part of what is changing in me. Death is all around me and I do not think I can cope any more.

I rang Harold's wife and Linda's daughter, arranged to see them to plan things. As I spoke with each of them on the phone, there was another conversation going on in my head, which reminded me that dying in your old age does not necessarily mean that the death is painless. That often the final few months or even years can be full of suffering, that some people starve to death because the medication and machines keep them sort of functioning but not really actually alive. That it was possible that Harold and Linda had died in this way. Or maybe that they had been forgotten in a nursing home, faceless, nameless, silent occupants of an institutional arm chair, gazing vacantly at mindless television, the sound muted or deafeningly loud, depending on who had got hold of the remote most recently. All sorts of pictures swirled through my head, of people I had known, reduced to statues, only a small trail of dribble reminding you they are alive, or the remains of breakfast, carelessly left on their face by an overworked or indifferent staff member. The worst was a bed ridden man, sheets soaked in sweat and urine, only changed because I had gone and shouted at the manager, waving the pictures on my phone to emphasize my point.

Times of visits agreed, I hung up and tried to distract myself from the gloom, to ignore the Weasel's snide voice. I managed to populate a rota with the easy bits, duplicating the pattern of who did what reading what week of the month. But unsurprisingly this was not enough to stop the argument in my head. Fortunately, it was time to go and see John instead, so that got me moving.

"Afternoon, Father."

"Hi John. You're looking okay today. How do you feel?"

"I've felt better, but also worse. Slept okay. I used to miss having no one else in bed to hug, but that stopped months ago, so I'm already getting used to it."

That was a stunningly honest comment. Hardly anyone is that clear about the pain. It is always these little things that hurt the most. Walking into the supermarket that you went to together every week, stopping at a favourite cafe or restaurant and the waiter, who knows you by sight if not by name, asking after your wife. A bench with a favourite view, a familiar joint routine you now complete alone. The little things, the glue that holds a couple together. Once these go, it is no wonder life shatters and there are shards everywhere, waiting to be joined together. It was not just Marion's beloved cup that was broken.

John offered me the inevitable mug of tea, which I was grateful for as I had the beginnings of a caffeine withdrawal headache coming on.

Settling into the same chairs we always sat in, we began with the business that needed attending to. "I need to check with you about the music for coming in and going out of church. Did you decide on CDs?"

"Yeah, I have. We'll come in to *Yesterday*. I think it fits well. I probably will want a place to hide. But got to face up to it. Got to do it. And we'll go out to *Imagine*."

I had been writing these down and looked up startled. "Imagine there's no heaven... Really?"

John folded his arms, and stared at me silently, a faint smile on his face, daring me to refuse his atheist joke.

"Really, John? Is that what Marion would have wanted?"

"Probably not, but I want it. I really don't think there is anything else left of her. There is no other place. You'll tell everyone she's safe with Jesus in the service, and I want a chance to put across a different point of view."

A tiny, hidden, bit of me that whispered "he's got a point." I sometimes call him the Weasel, because that's what he sounds like, a scoffing, malicious, doubter, full of weasel words. "Imagine you're wasting your life. Imagine there's

24

nothing more. It's easy if you try. Imagine its all just pie in the sky when you die and that it's a lie."

I was tempted, if I'm honest, tempted to accept the pointlessness of it all, tempted to accept my position as a waste of time, a social worker with no training, a man in a dress who stands at the front of funerals spouting platitudes, while everyone else crosses their fingers, kind of hopes its true, and wonders whether granny really is looking down on them as a star, and whether that is a good thing or not. But somewhere within me was a bit of professional pride, a bit of the militant who wants to insist that even if I was not quite sure what it all meant, I had to somehow remain loyal to the teaching of the church.

"Okay, John, how about this. We'll go out to *Imagine*, but only if I can introduce it with an explanation of why you've chosen it. Something about how you and she had very different understandings of faith, and that you want to reflect that difference through the choice of music?"

"Sure, be my guest." John, magnanimous in victory, permitted this with a wave of his mug of tea, from which he took a swig before explaining further.

"Marion and I did talk a lot about this, you know. Its not just me having a dig, or being a rebel. We talked about what if there was and wasn't a heaven. What if I was wrong, what if she was wrong. She was so honest about dying and about how she was both terrified and excited. I didn't really understand it all, but for me, being able to play that song at that point is a way of marking those conversations."

I had to know more about this, but was not really sure if it was okay to ask. It felt too nosy, to intrusive into the private goodbyes of a couple who loved each other even if they disagreed about Jesus. Maybe I would find out about it one day, but today it seemed too rude to ask. Instead I showed him the service sheet. He glanced at it and handed it back with a nod of approval. "Looks fine."

"Okay, John, we'll finish with *Imagine*. Sometime I'd love to know more about what you and Marion said, but maybe after the funeral would be better. I think that is everything sorted out, so thank you. Was the funeral director okay? Was it Clive?"

"Yeah, it was. He's a good bloke. Good at his job. Happy to do what you want him to. But the florist, she's irritating me."

"How so?" Time for a biscuit I decided. I could be here a while.

"Oh, faffing and fussing and wanting me to decide exactly which flowers. I just told her, a nice bouquet. Don't ask me for details. I know colours but I don't know flowers, and have no intention of learning now."

"Fair enough. I'm quite ignorant myself." Another bite of the biscuit.

"Another thing that annoys me," John said, taking a sip of his tea. "Is that people are so stupid in what they say."

"What do you mean?" I was slightly wary of where this conversation was going. People can say daft things to the recently bereaved, and I know that a few of my congregation are champions at foot-in-mouth competitions. Was this going to be some other pastoral tangle for me to gently unknot?

"Well," John said. "Take 'I'm sorry that you've lost Marion?' I haven't lost her. I know exactly where she is. She's in the undertaker's fridge. Or what about 'passed away?' Has she really passed anywhere? Why can't people just say, 'It's a bloody shame Marion's dead?' That's what I want to hear."

"Well, you're right, it is a bloody shame Marion's dead," I replied. John's never heard me come close to swearing before, so that took him by surprise. The milli-second of silence gave me permission to keep going. "The thing is, people like me spend quite a lot of their time talking about death and with people who have recently had someone die." I was choosing my words carefully, and had nearly said 'with people who had lost someone,' but that would have been more fuel to the fire of John's frustration.

"But most people," I went on, "most people do not know what to say about death. In fact, most people are a bit scared of death, don't really want to talk about death, and so go for vague, less harsh, softer, ways of talking about it. You are right that it can be frustrating, but I'm afraid that's just people."

John sipped more tea and thought for a bit. I decided that it was time for a second chocolate biscuit. Normally one would be my rule, but this was tough going. Food for the brain, is chocolate. The cloying, melting sensation in my mouth was some small comfort, giving me a flutter of courage. At least, that's what I keep telling my growing waistline. There was more that I felt I had to say.

"Thing is, John, we hide death away these days. We hide people in nursing homes. We pretend they're not going to die, or that they're too ill to notice. Or leave them in hospital, with the white sheets and bleep, bleep of machines, pretending it is all under control. Sometimes the staff are wonderful, other times they are not. Sometimes the care is amazing, sometimes substandard, a norovirus explosion of death by failure to wash hands."

"You do have a way with words, sometimes, Paul." John looked at me, slightly taken aback by my outburst. "But I'm glad you're not hiding things away, and I know how lucky we were that Marion was at home for most of the time, even if the last two weeks were in the hospice. It was one of the good places, was that hospice. I guess so many people make donations to them, they can afford to keep it clean and employ good staff."

"Petty much," I confirmed. "Not everywhere is that good. When Mary was pregnant with Annabelle, there were several nursing homes that I just would not go to. Too worried about what I might pass on to her. It saddens me to realise that we forget human beings that easily."

"Life is cruel, that's for sure." John nodded.

We talked a bit more, mainly about John's memories of Marion, or about the weather or the football, a rambling sometimes profound, sometimes inane half hour. Always nagging in the back of my mind was the thought, "What if John's got a point, and there is no heaven? What if he's right and you are wrong?"

Horses and Weasels

Clip clop, clip clop. There is something unbelievably fitting about a horse drawn hearse. Not especially good for the bank balance of course, and not a choice many people make, but somehow appropriate. A reminder of times gone by, when the pace of life was slower, when people were happier talk about death perhaps, because it was around far more. These days, death is so often clinical, white, tidy and silent. It used to be far messier, dirtier, louder. At least that's what I tell myself.

I remember my gran talking about when her little brother died of pneumonia. It was a harsh winter; he was not the only case. Nowhere near as bad as the Spanish flu of 1918 mind you, she'd added. But for her, death at a young age, while tragic, was also normal. There may have been a horse and cart at funerals, but nothing grand. It was a working animal and someone doing you a favour, the milkman perhaps, or if you were less fortunate, the coal man, whose cart was never as clean.

There is something about the horses. The clean windows of the carriage, the plumes in the horses' tackle. Maybe it is what it says: here is someone we love, whom we want to give the best sendoff we can. Clip clop, clip clop, stop and look, doff your cap, pay your respects, say goodbye. I like horse drawn funerals as I call them.

Actually I used to enjoy taking all funerals, but since Mum's death, it has got so much harder. I say "I am the resurrection and the life" in a loud clear voice as I lead a coffin into church. Then "Really? Is he? You sure?" the Weasel doubter scoffs in my inner ear as I walk to the front of the church. "Is that what will happen to your Mum? He loved her so much he let her decay like a shriveled prune." My pet Weasel, as I think of him, pops up every time I take a funeral. Kind of cramps my style when I am supposed to be helping people mourn and say their last goodbyes with dignity.

The Weasel likes to remind me about what happened to Mum. As he puts it, dementia is a thief, a right cruel bastard at that. He does not just smash and grab, leaving you with a horrible mess to tidy up and recover from. No, he takes a bit, leaves a bit, comes back for it later. Even crueler, he occasionally gives a bit back. Only for a while, mind you, little bits that he soon reclaims. The thief Dementia stole my mother from me, over fourteen cruel months. You cannot chase him away or arrest him, he just comes and takes what he wants.

Dementia starts quietly, gently, a skilled pickpocket almost. He just lifts a few memories, maybe a little bit of functionality. Short term memory is one of his favourite treasures. "I can remember playing in Victoria Park as an eight year old girl, but I have no idea if I ate lunch," Mum said to me one day on the phone. I was in the habit of trying to have a brief chat most days, and thought nothing of it at the time. But now I think it was Dementia's first theft, neat and tidy, a clean in and out job.

He started to steal regularly from then onwards. Just a little bit at a time, a memory here, a bit of confidence there, maybe a fine motor skill as well, just to rob a bit more dignity. Forgetting if she had eaten became a common problem, and she started to put on weight. Unsurprising really, most of us would get fat if we ate five or six meals a day and did not really go out much at all. She had to start writing notes to herself, with the date and time, saying things like "Tuesday 14th March. 8am. Ate breakfast." I bought her a big whiteboard and put it up in the kitchen. That worked for a while. But then she forgot to write things down, or forgot to write the full date, or lost the pen, or any number of myriad ways in which what seemed like a neat solution suddenly became another source of stress.

The biggest problem was that Mum was too old to move house. She had stayed too long where she was. She was not ready to go into full nursing care, but the stress of moving would have been too much for her. She lived about an hour's drive from me, so I could not go that often, as there are not many working days for a vicar with a spare three hours in them. Home helps were fantastic at the early stages. Gladys, her personal shopper, was an angel of mercy, getting her food every week. Once things got a bit worse and she had a visit from a care worker morning and night the situation improved for a while.

But Mum could not always remember who these people were. The same lady came most of the time—Agnieszka, I think her name was—nice lass from Poland trying to make a better life for herself in Britain. But even when she was working a full week, that was only five or six days. When she had a holiday, who knew who was coming (even the agency seemed unsure at times). Mum certainly had no clue who these people were. Waking up to find a "big black man, Paul, terrifying he was" had let himself in while she was still asleep at eight o'clock one Wednesday morning. It was nearly enough to send her straight to her grave. He was just doing his job, poor bloke, but maybe not very well, and certainly not well supervised.

All this plays through my mind when what I am supposed to be doing is helping other people grieve. Means I am really not very good at it, at least it makes me think I must be bad at it.

So what should I do? I have to take funerals. It is an essential part of my role. Essential because the income it generates is useful for St Mark's, helping keep the lights on and the temperature at least a bit above uncomfortable and hovering in bearable. And it is part of being an Anglican vicar. It is what we do. We're available to take the funeral of anyone in our area whose family might want us to. Not that many families do want us to these days, but about once every ten days people do. So maybe thirty times this year, the Weasel is going to pop out and scoff.

I can clearly remember starting doing them as a curate. I was scared of messing up my first funeral. The boss had been kind; it was an eighty-six year old, much loved grandmother.

She had died at home after a long illness. The family were all ready for her to die. "It was a merciful relief" was the comment from one of the relatives (can't remember who). Small family, just a service in the crem. Very straightforward. A good first solo flight. Still nerve wracking and terrifying, of course. It was at 2:30pm, and I don't think I actually managed to get anything done that morning, just reading and re-reading the service. Checking my notes, making sure I got every detail of her life right. That I was word perfect with my eulogy. I timed it all, playing the hymns on a CD, making sure it would fit comfortably within the twenty minutes I was aiming for. My first run through was a rushed and shoddy fifteen minutes. Slow down, man, it's a funeral, not a sprint. Second attempt was better, a solid eighteen. Third was nineteen. Fourth was nineteen. Time to try and do something else. Failed at that one.

I left the house at one pm. I was at the crem by 1:20. Too embarrassed to go into the vestry yet, I just sat in the shade in my car, waiting, waiting, waiting. I went to get robed at 2:10, was outside at 2:20. The service is a blur now. As far as I know it was fine. I cannot even remember the woman's name any more. Actually, I'm not even sure if she was eighty-six. I just made that up as I was reminiscing. She was old, it was uncomplicated, and after completing a dozen in the first four months of my job, I found I enjoyed taking funerals. That first family were grateful, invited me back to the pub with them afterwards. I went, relieved it was over. Had a cup of tea, had my arm twisted for a whiskey. When the double came, looking suspiciously like a treble, I realised I would have to walk home, and refused the offer of a second glass.

Funerals were okay, enjoyable even. The pleasure of a difficult job well done, a family helped through a tough time. A professional at work. All that pride.

I hate them now. The Weasel is there every time. He comes to visit the families with me, makes his suggestions, gets in the way. I shout at him on the way home in the car sometimes. He's even reduced me to tears once. It was the morning after Mum's funeral. I had taken a few days compassionate leave between her death and the funeral, to get the details sorted. I had come back to too much to do, a grey rainy February morning, after a sleepless, restless night I looked at myself in the mirror in the hall, adjusting my dog collar, and I heard him say, "You know all this is a waste of time? There's no future after death. That is it. You're giving people false hope, a hope your mother was never even able to comprehend. You're alone now, an orphan, spouting crap to gullible old ladies so you can get their money when they die." The rolling tears made me wonder if he was right.

He has been quiet for most of the time I spent with John, but as I walked back home from John's house, that Wednesday afternoon, the second visit after Marion's death, he had enjoyed himself immensely. "Imagine there's no heaven. Go on, Paul, imagine it. You've been wasting your time all these years. Your mum went to nothing, food for the worms. True of your dad as well. Will be true for Marion, only they're having her cremated, so there won't be anything left for even the worms to eat."

He was back again today as well. Friday morning, a dull day, threatening rain in a classic English, lazy, actually I probably cannot be bothered sort of way. The kind of day that makes you want to pack a coat and then realise you did not need it because the rain never actually comes. Here I was in the front seat of a stretch limo, watching the horse drawn hearse in front of me, enjoying the rhythm of the hooves on the tarmac. The service in church had gone fine. It had been a small ceremony, only thirty or so mourners. I had given a brief eulogy, including a very brief history of Trevor's life. The family had told me virtually nothing of his life. They were uncertain of his schooling, unclear of his first jobs, sure he liked fishing and action films, no other hobbies, no particular memories or jokes or catchphrases. All in all, nothing special, a decent enough job from me, the Weasel offering his running commentary about how this was an equal waste of time, that Trevor Williams was also just a bit more rotting meat soon to become dust and ashes. "There is nothing, remember, there is no heaven, nothing after this."

No exactly what you want to have running through your head as you try to comfort a bereaved family. "Death can feel very painful at this time, but Jesus says I am the resurrection and the life," were the words coming out of my mouth. "And he's quite wrong, there is no life after death idiot" was the thought running through my brain.

How can I do this job when I am not sure if I even believe in any of it any more?

☐

Goodbye Marion

I was convinced Marion's funeral was going to be amongst the hardest I have ever taken. Funerals for babies and children are always difficult, those for adults who had died in tragic circumstances equally so. This time, it was more about what was going on in my head than the circumstances of Marion's death. The Weasel was in an evil mood from the night before. Mary had spotted the signs at tea time. She is really good at reading my moods, having learnt the hard way, through years of bitter experience. When I am stressed I tend to say what I think a bit too quickly and a bit too sharply. Why is it that our families suffer from our own failures? Mary has borne more than her fair share of my upset over the years. She was telling me about the literacy lesson she had taught earlier today. How some of the children had really engaged well, imagining their desert islands, which sounded quite luxurious to me. My favourite was the one that had broadband and a tree that grew chocolate biscuits. As usual Adam and Karl had refused to imagine anything much. "Theres an eye-land. Sand Palm tres. Boring." was all Adam managed to write.

I grunted, managed a half smile.

"What's got into you?" she asked me as we stood from the table to begin tidying the kitchen. "You barely said a word at tea. Jack really wanted to tell you about the second team football match and you barely showed any interest. I know you aren't the biggest footie fan in the world, but it's important to him, and he needs you to be more interested."

"I know," I sighed. "I know. I should have been honest with him—and all of you. I'm so wound up about Marion's funeral tomorrow that I don't think I can pay any attention to anything else. The Weasel is starting to whine already, which is earlier than usual."

"Why do you give your doubts such a name?" She stopped wiping the table to look at me, her exasperation clear from her face, frustration beaming from each of her bewitching green eyes.

I told Mary about the Weasel right after Mum died. She told me I was an idiot, and that naming it was going to make it worse. I managed—just—to not reply. As time has gone on, I am starting to think she was—as usual—right. But the Weasel is with me now, and I do not think I will ever get away from him.

I finished loading the dishwasher and then when to find Jack. He was slumped in the living room, more than filling our two-seater sofa, his feet hanging over the edge. I'm sure they're making fourteen-year olds bigger these days. He was lost in swiping on his tablet. Looked like some kind of a puzzle. At least there were only limited explosions and killing.

"Jack, son, I'm sorry."

An apology out of nowhere was enough to break into his zone of concentration. He looked up, forehead wrinkled in puzzlement. Why was Dad apologising to him? "What for?"

"For not really listening at tea time. Mum's just reminded me of how rude I was. I always have a go at you when you're rude, so its only fair that I get told when I am as well." I collapsed into an armchair, fighting the urge to explain, to unload my problems onto fourteen-year old shoulders no where near strong enough to hold them. Jack was quite upset when Grandpa Richard died, and talked about it. But I really have no idea what he thought about Nanny Margaret dying. He has never said, which almost certainly means it was hard for him. Even if it was not, there is no need to give him any of my issues.

"Tell me about the footie match."

The puzzle called him back, and his head went down, his fingers started moving. But I was worth the rest of his attention, and he told me that they'd been playing the All Saints Academy second team, who were three places below them in the league. They remained three places below them in the league, because Sam Hargreaves had scored two cracking goals, one with an assist from Jack. All his mates had thanked him as well as Sam, recognising his contribution. Jack is much more sporty than me. That is not really a complement, as there are probably goalposts which are more sporty than me, and which have scored more goals than me, though either accident or design. But being praised by your peers is water to the thirsty soul of any teenager, and I was glad that Jack was fitting in with his mates.

"Well done Jack. I'm probably going to take Saturday afternoon off this week, so do you want to go somewhere to celebrate?"

"Can we go and get some cakes from that posh bakery?"

"Sure, if we buy take out, as it's too close to the end of the month for me to afford four drinks as well as four Patisserie Valerie cakes."

"Sound Dad. I ain't fussed by the drinks. I just want one of those Strawberry Gateaux. If we bring it home, I can add squirty cream as well."

Jack grinned at me, and I grinned back. We could both hear Mary's "that's disgusting" in response to Jack's over consumption of cream. Aiding and abetting such gluttony seemed like a suitable apology.

"It's a deal. I'll take you early afternoon. Now I'm going to look over my notes for tomorrow."

'What's happening?" Jack wasn't really interested, the call of the tablet getting stronger now the promise of cake and cream was secured.

"Oh, a funeral. You remember Marion, don't you?" Even keeping my voice calm and measured was an effort.

"Yeah, so that's tomorrow. I kind of miss her. She was nice." High praise from the boy, but I guess Marion's regular Christmas gift of a decent selection box helped win my kids' affections.

I read over the notes, which was a stupid thing to do. Reading the notes meant reading the eulogy, which meant reminding myself of the tragedy of her death, of my unanswered prayers, of my nagging doubts and questions. I should have just watched a pre-recorded Top Gear or one of those travel programmes and left the read through till the morning. But having looked once meant I read it all three times, and then found myself crying in my study while the Weasel crowed in my head: "See, no god, no future, death is just the end, you live, die, then rot. That's where your Mum is, that's where your Dad is. You're wasting your time with your pointless words. You have no idea at all of what will happen next. So why do you bother. You're just a slightly inept, untrained social worker, who may be making a difference to one or two, but that's it."

Once he starts, he's really hard to drown out. He was even worse the night before Mum's funeral than on the morning after it. I kept seeing the image of her, wizened and wrinkled in her final few days, no longer capable of any intelligent speech, screeching with rage at me for keeping her locked up or stealing her chocolates or hiding her slippers, or whatever misdemeanour Dementia was telling her I was guilty of.

I slept badly the night before Marion's funeral, clinging on to Mary like a koala hugging a tree in a monsoon, desperate to avoid drowning in the battering rain of grief and doubt. In the morning I was bedraggled and bewildered, not in great shape for the emotional roller coaster to come.

The following morning was a grey one. A slight breeze, swaying the tree tops. Not especially warm. Dull, depressing, perfectly apt for my mood and the events of eleven am. I was glad it was a morning funeral. I would have been a wreck if it had been in the afternoon. There was time to have a decent breakfast, say Morning Prayer, make sure church was completely tidy, a cup of coffee at ten am and then back to church.

The car park was already filling up, little clumps of mourners like black mushrooms. Church was virtually empty when I went in at about 10:15. People never come in beforehand, even the regulars normally wait outside. A few venerable souls were inside, legs not strong enough to stand for that long. Mrs Travis was in her usual seat. No one else was ever allowed to sit in Mrs Travis' seat, and she has been known to arrive an hour early to ensure this sacred tradition continues. She was suitably ensconced, comfortably observing the to-and-fro of setting up, the arranging of the trestles for the coffin, the putting out of the RESERVED sign, authoritative capital letters daring you to defy them. Caroline Short was there too, which was odd. She can hardly have known Marion, but had come early and taken a seat next to Mrs Travis, chatting to her while they waited.

The hearse was two minutes early, pulling into the car park at 10:58am, a single limousine behind it. John had told me he wanted "to do it properly but not waste money," and was being true to his word. Marshes were conducting the funeral. They're a good firm. I think I may have recommended them to Marion at some point. They're neither the cheapest nor the most expensive, but the people are wonderful professionals, sensitive but not slushy, interested in bereaved families as people, not as business propositions. Clive Marsh is a gentleman. He really looks the part, smart three-piece suit, no hat ("too pretentious"), or silver topped cane ("daft idea"). Shiny shoes, clean-shaven, everything in hand. A calm unrushed, respectful pro. His presence at a funeral even silences the Weasel for a while.

He had been quite quiet so far this morning, had the Weasel. He was probably a bit tired from last night, and he poked his head out of his burrow just as I was shaking Clive's hand. That's another thing I like about Clive. He doesn't do the "pass the brown envelope with the cheque in it at the door" move. There are one or companies who do that, and it is so annoying. I do have to be paid, but there's a time and a place and just before things start really is the wrong one, especially if I drop a five hundred pound cheque in a muddy puddle because I was not expecting to be given it.

"Morning Clive. I think we'll be a full church, so let's start promptly."

"Sure, Paul. She was well loved, it seems."

Clive marshalled his bearers, all pros, all used to doing this smartly and sensitively. By two minutes past I was leading a long snaking line of black clad mourners into St Mark's, as the strains of *Yesterday* echoed through the church.

Now I need a place to hide away. Oh I believe in yesterday.

I certainly do, I thought. "Did you know that the original words were going to be 'Scrambled eggs'?" the Weasel asked me incredulously, actually behaving himself for once.

"Yes, I did," I replied. "Now you shut up and let me get on with my job."

And you know what, he did.

Small Shoots

Something changed that day. It was a tiny shoot. The kind of small plant that a passing slug swallows in one go. But it was a green shoot. Since Mum died, the field of my faith had been scorched and burnt. The Weasel had wandered all over it, scattering salt to stop any new crop of belief growing, and he had been fairly successful. I was a vicar who no longer believed in life after death, a professional follower of Jesus Christ who no longer stood for what he stood for. I was a good enough professional to have hidden this field from public view. The hedges and fences around my faith field were high enough that only a select few had any idea of what was within. Vicars always perform. Some of them are frustrated (or frustrating) actors who went for the mundane security of a regular role with a free house and guaranteed money every month, not the risk of trying to make it big. People outsource believing to you, make you become the reservoir of hope they can go to to drink the water of life from when they need it. Did I actually have to believe in order to fulfil this function, or could I just go on pretending?

Perhaps I could have carried on indefinitely in this way. You can play a role for a long time, if you're a good actor, and taking a funeral could just be another role, a piece of professional acting for the benefit of the mourners. But Christians are supposed to be authentic, not hypocrites. The word hypocrite comes from a Greek word that means actor. I do not think I am supposed to act like a Christian, but to actually live like one. The problem is, actually doing it was so hard. I can pretend to be a Christian easily enough. You know, lead the service, the prayer meeting, appear concerned when people tell me their problems, offer to pray for them, actually say a prayer for them if I remember, all of that sort of stuff. But actually be sure that when I died there really was a Creator God who was going to sort out all of the mess, heal all the hurts, dry all the tear-filled eyes. That was a bit harder. Actually, that was an awful lot harder. So much harder. I walked into St Mark's that day, fairly sure that this was one of the last funerals I would do, one of the last services I would take. I had no idea what to do next, but in my present frame of mind I did not think it was at all likely that I was going to be a vicar for much longer. The idea sitting there passively beeping people's shopping from store to bag was starting to become a whole lot more attractive.

But when I walked out, Marion's coffin behind me, it felt like this was one of many more to come. I am not really sure what happened at Marion's funeral. Maybe it was the fact that I managed to shut out the Weasel for the whole of the thirty-minute service. Maybe it was the voices of the congregation singing about "No fear in death" and "In life, in death, abide with me" like they actually meant it and believed it. Maybe it was the fact that at the end of the service I found myself saying this:

"Most of you know that John and Marion had very different views about faith. Marion was a devoted follower of Jesus Christ and a pillar of this church. John is much more sceptical than that. He and I have talked about faith a few times. John and Marion talked about faith many more times, and neither convinced the other to completely change their mind. John wanted to somehow mark this fact, this important aspect of his relationship with Marion in her funeral. And that is why he has chosen *Imagine* to be the song we listen to as we exit the church. 'Imagine there's no heaven, it's easy if you try.' For John that is all too easy. For Marion, next to impossible. I do not know where any of you stand. Maybe closer to John, or maybe closer to Marion. The thing I have learnt from both of them is the importance of being honest about what we believe, and staying in close relationship even when we profoundly disagree."

I paused at that point, mainly because I wanted to try and understand what I had said, but also to give everyone else a chance to absorb it. Clearly no one was going to heckle just before the final commendation at a funeral, but you can still get disapproval. There was none. I had been honest, aired one of my doubts (although not honestly, so a bit more hypocrisy really) and survived. Maybe there was space to talk about the truth.

"And now, let us commend Marion to the mercy of God, our maker and our redeemer."

The closing rhythm of the service. The final prayers, the awkward manoeuvre as the pall bearers turn the coffin around with as much dignity as possible. The solemn walk out, as John Lennon suggested to us we were all wasting our time. It was strangely comforting for that possibility to be out in the open. Comforting because I felt I could say to the Weasel that Lennon was wrong. I did say it, he told me I was stupid, and clearly Lennon had a point. I told him I no longer cared what he thought, and went to sit in the front of the hearse and chat about the football with Larry, the driver, as we made our way slowly to the crem to reverently dispose of Marion's mortal remains.

Larry was in a positive mood that morning, which is not always the case. Sometimes he is quite surly, refusing to talk about anything much. Today was a good day though, perhaps because there had been some decent football last night, and tonight there was a very real possibility that Manchester United would be beaten by Barcelona and denied further progress through the Champions' League. Like many Scousers, Larry is as happy when Man U are being beaten as when the Red Men are doing well.

We had a pleasant fifteen minutes discussing the chances of a Barca victory. The advantage of being in the hearse is that there is no need to keep a reverent silence. When I travel in the front seat of a limo, I tend to just watch the world go by, as the family normally do not want to talk about anything much, and it seems unprofessional to be discussing the footie in the front while they grieve in the back.

Traffic was kind and we made it to the crem with a few minutes to spare. Clive knows how to fill in the time at a situation like this, and the hearse stopped as soon as we had pulled into the drive that led up to the crem. He and I got out and we walked slowly up to the chapel, taking our time, ensuring that when we arrived at the door it was exactly 12 noon. I smiled at Clive. "I think you've done this before."

He grinned back, a professional pleased with a job well done. "Once or twice."

He then disappeared inside to make sure everything was ready for us. I also slipped into the vestry. The chapel seemed quiet. I eased the door open gently. It was empty.

I went in, heading for the front, turning the crucifix around, so a plain wooden cross would greet the mourners. Many Scousers are not religious, but they can still have strong Protestant views, and for some, anything that smacks of Catholicism is to be avoided at all costs. No candles, a plain cross, no crucifix, no crossing yourself or kneeling, Queen and country, all of that. There are parts of Liverpool where the Orange Lodge is still loud and proud and they make sure you do things the way they want them.

The curtains were open. The cross was showing. No candles in sight. I was ready.

Clive reappeared, the crem attendant following behind.

"All set?"

"Yeah, good to go."

Clive opened the doors and he and I went out to greet John and his family, who were standing just to the left of the doors. A large crowd was gathering behind them. A few cars were still passing, heading for the car park.

"Let's give it a few minutes," I suggested. "Make sure everyone has had a chance to park."

"Okay," John agreed. "Is there a toilet?"

"Let me show you." Clive directed him.

John was only a few minutes. When he came back out, his eyes looked slightly red. I didn't say anything. The crem toilet is a good a place as any to shed a few tears.

We processed in, Eva Cassidy welcoming us. I read the Psalm, invited people to stand again, said the committal and then closed the curtains as I reminded everyone present about "ashes to ashes and dust to dust." As usual I kept my finger on the curtain closing button far too long. They were closed when I still had two sentences of the prayer left, but I prefer to move as little as possible, and did not want to draw attention to the mechanics of what I was doing.

Since we had another fifteen minutes before the chapel was next in use, I told people they could sit and listen to the final piece of music, and leave when they were ready. John has picked a lovely piece, *Bridge over troubled water*. Again it was Eva; apparently she was one of Marion's favourite singers, he told me later. One outing of the Beatles was enough he had decided. Marion like Eva more than John, and he had the song he really wanted in the church. I stayed a bit longer than normal, enjoying the music, before going out to stand and wait for the mourners to file past.

Some shook my hand "Nice service, Father." "Thanks, lad." The usual. Some made no eye contact, just heading straight for the smokers' corner. A few minutes after we had finished, Clive appeared with the flowers. John said he did not want them, and that they could just stay here.

"Rather they rotted here than in my house. Saves me having to clear up. Let's go, please," he asked. "I'll see everyone at the wake."

Slugs and Bugs

Small shoots are very vulnerable. Slugs and snails love to eat them up, or so my very limited experience and expertise as a gardener tells me. I remember when Jack was about two we tried to grow some sunflowers for him. The first stage went fine: we planted them in a large pot, watered them regularly, but not too often. That was quite a challenge, because Jack really got into watering. As with many toddlers, anything involving pouring water was wonderful in his world, and I think if he had had his way, he would have poured those sunflowers their own personal ocean. But Mary was a wise mother: she devolved responsibility for watering to me, and specifically to me as part of the bedtime routine. Every day, once I had read him a story, and before he went up for his bath, Jack and I would water his sunflowers.

After just a few weeks tiny shoots began to emerge. I was pleased with our progress as gardeners. Jack and I were actually growing something together. He loved watering, but was following the rules, only watering a bit, only watering once each day, despite his desperate desire to give them as much to drink as his baby sister was being breastfed. The shoots grew to be a good three inches tall. New life emerging from the soil, into a world full of peril.

Following the instructions on the packet, we planted those sunflowers outside. I think most of them lasted one night. A tasty snack for a passing snail or slug or some such similar animal. I had to try and explain to Jack that his sunflowers were gone, and that we would have to start again. He did not really understand, and we were due to go on holiday in less than a month, so it was not really the time to start again. The only life those sunflowers had outside lasted less than a day.

The shoots of my new found positivity about funerals lasted about as long. Maybe slightly longer. I was in a good mood when I got back from Marion's wake.

"I'm home!" I called out as I came in. Mary came out and gave me a hug.

"Oh, good, you're back. I've missed you," she informed my collarbone.

I was confused. "This is very pleasant, but why the sudden affection?" I gave her bottom a slight squeeze, just because.

She jumped, as she always does, and lifted her head to smile at me. "Well, that, for starters. For the past year at least, every time you have come back from a funeral you have been horrible. There is no way you would have called out a greeting, never mind squeeze my bottom. Which is a shame, as I missed both of those." She gave me a flirty smile.

She had wanted to come to Marion's funeral, but taking time off work was difficult; the head would let her take time for a relative's funeral, but "someone from church" was not quite close enough.

I sighed, deeply, suddenly realising exactly how many people I was hurting exactly how much. Death takes so much more than we can imagine.

"Yeah, I'm sorry. It went well today. Fewer doubts, less rage in my head, I guess. I think it was the honesty of John choosing *Imagine* as the exit music from church. Made me realise that it might be okay to have doubts."

"Course it is. I've been trying to tell you that for months now. 'Imagine there's no heaven, it's easy if you try.' I think its been a bit too easy for you, hasn't it? Were you just glad someone else voiced it?"

"Something like that. I think it was just nice to be able to talk honestly about how John and Marion had different views, but loved each other, and that implicit in the complexity of their relationship is the fact that none of us is entirely one hundred percent sure of what will happen when we die. I guess I just needed to be able to air some of that, although a funeral is hardly the place for the vicar to indulge in too much navel gazing." I tightened my arms again and hugged her silently for a minute.

Hugs can be so restorative, contact with another person, reminding you that the faceless death of funerals is not all there is to life. Not by a long way. Part of me wanted that hug to go on and on. But then duty called. He always calls.

"Can I have a cup of tea please? I'm going to say hi to the kids and then go delete emails."

"Okay. You might want to read some of them first. The kids are in their rooms—staying out of the way in case you were grumpy again. I'm the first line of defence." She smiled again, returned the favour of a squeezed bottom, and then headed for the kitchen.

That comment caught me unawares. First line of defence? Then I remembered. A few weeks ago I had come back from a funeral in a foul mood and had shouted at Jack and Annabelle, just for being relaxed and flippant as they watched telly while waiting for tea. It was entirely my bad mood, nothing to do with either of them. It had cost me a trip to Pizza Hut to make amends, a well-deserved punishment.

Death takes more than you imagine, and often from people who have done nothing to cause you any pain. I had to get better at controlling my anger. Maybe these green shoots would change things. I felt optimistic that they might. I went to find them upstairs, shouting cheerily that "It's okay, you don't need to hide, I'm in a good mood," as I went upstairs.

"Cat Woman called again today," Annabelle informed me.

"I'm really not sure you should call her that." I smiled.

"What," she protested, palms up, weighing the options of insult and amusement. "She calls round every few weeks, asking for 50p for a tin of cat food. I don't know her name. What else should I call her?"

"Fair enough," I sighed. She had a point, and I quite liked the name, so I could not really complain. "What did you do?"

"Gave her 50p of course. Got it from your change pot." She grinned at me, daring me to give her the "don't give money to people who knock and ask" lecture.

"Okay," I ruffled her hair. "So long as it's never more than a quid, you understand?"

"Sure, dad. If there's that much money in there, I might buy myself some chocolate." Another cheeky grin. She was mining my good mood for all the gold she could get, unsure of when the next rock fall was coming.

Jack was actually doing homework. Today had been fine, apparently. The usual had happened, whatever that was. "Want to get this done before tea dad."

Enough said, leave the boy in peace. Do not block the homework train. It takes so long to get in rolling, I would be in serious trouble if I derailed it or slowed it down.

I went to my study. I did actually read many of the emails that were clamouring for my attention. Only read part of the subject line of some, but others were given more detailed, proper scrutiny, and replied to before they were filed or deleted. Inbox zero is one of those mythical states that I rarely achieve. Occasionally if I invest several hours I manage it just before I go on holiday, but normally only by cheating and creating a "deal with when I'm back" folder to move the stubborn ones into.

I had a rare evening free of meetings, no urgent pastoral visits to do and I rough idea of what I wanted to say the following Sunday. All in all, the perfect combination for a night off. Mary was also home, I was in a good mood, definitely an opportunity for some family time. We played a bit of "Christian monopoly" which is where all debts are forgiven, players club together to help each other out rather than ruthlessly building personal property empires with which to annihilate each other. It can often descend into farce and there is never a winner, more just a chance for a bit of family banter really. Annabelle, who hates making others suffer, loves this version. Jack thinks it's a bit silly, but humours us. We lasted about an hour of playing, before other duties called.

The shoots of my hopeful sunflower were doing just fine when I went to bed.

I slept well, but the next day was not so good. The morning was fine. I said Morning Prayer as usual, actually felt like God and I were on decent speaking terms for a change. I was in the mood for the conversation, brought up a few concerns I had about folks in the parish, my general sense of unease about the wider world situation and also a bit of time trying to concentrate on saying thank you, something I have never been very good at.

I spent the morning writing my sermon and getting everything else ready for Sunday, the powerpoint and notice sheet and so on, nothing difficult, all stuff that at least half the congregation think appear by magic. Nothing to trouble the sunflower there.

But in the afternoon I had to go and see Mrs Griffiths, Harold's widow, and a slug came by to gobble up my green shoots of hope.

She had been destroyed by his death. There really is no other word to describe it. Utterly and completely destroyed. He was her whole world. Married for sixty-one years, childhood sweethearts who had waited until they both had jobs before marrying and getting a family. "We didn't want me to get pregnant before we could afford to care for our baby, and so we waited for probably two years longer than we really wanted to before we got married," she explained to me, just about controlling her tears. She talked about their courting, as she called it. About the flowers he bought her, the chocolates "even if he did end up eating most of them himself," and the long walks. They had enjoyed walking even in their older age, although the pace got slower and the distances shorter.

My small shoot of hope was shrivelling. I think the Weasel—I must not call him that—I think my doubts had never really gone. And watching this dear old lady cry broke my heart again. How can this be just? How can God love us when he takes one and leaves the other? I have done double funerals, of a husband and wife who were faithful together for sixty or even seventy years and died within a few weeks of each other. Though they are devastating for the children, there is also a certain rightness, a certain sense of divine providence of the Lord taking two inseparable people to be with him together. Why was Mrs Griffiths not given this privilege? Why was she left drowning in a sea of her own tears? The centre of attention now, but within two weeks, to be lonely and alone, unsure of how to do the shopping or deal with benefits, as "Harold always did all of that."

From the way she described him, Harold seemed like a lovely chap. Obviously she was biased, but she was also honest about the things that he did which were a bit annoying; his habit of buying an unnecessarily large number of garden gnomes for example. After you've got four, that is probably a surplus in most people's understanding of gnome quotas. For Harold is was not even a year's acquisition, nothing more. The Griffiths' family had over two hundred.

"I really don't know what to do about them. I always told myself that if he died first I would just chuck the lot of them, as they really get in the way. But they so remind me of him that part of me wants to keep them. But this old house is far too big just for me, and I can't put two hundred gnomes into a one bed flat can I?"

"I guess not. Maybe you could keep one or two and let everyone take one at the wake after the funeral?" I suggested, speaking without thinking, 'You know, kind of, take something to remember Harold by? I guess lots of people knew about his liking for gnomes?"

"Yes, maybe I will do that. I'll have to choose some for me, first, but maybe that is best. Thank you vicar, you're being so kind. Everyone is being so kind."

I did not feel kind. I felt more of a useless fraud. A rain of tears was falling in my own soul, and a slug was merrily chomping on my shoot of hope. I really could not believe any more. Maybe I would have to change career, find something that is less raw, less painful? But what could I do instead? Who would want to employ a man who has worked as a vicar for seventeen years and has never really had any other career? And how can I be a vicar if I cannot cope with taking funerals or talking to people who have been bereaved? □

Tailspin

Mary could tell that there was something wrong. We have been married for twenty-one years now, a year before I went off to theological college in fact, and she knows my moods.

After graduating from university I spent two years working for a church as a pastoral assistant, which is church-speak for general dogsbody. I got to do all the stuff that no one else really wanted to, and was given a room in a shared flat to live in and pocket money to pay for my food. The theory is that if you can survive two years of being bottom of the heap, then you probably do have what it takes to become a vicar. It worked for me. It certainly changed my life, not only because I got through selection, but also because Mary was another pastoral assistant, although she was only doing one year as a gap post university. She wanted to train as a teacher, and had got a deferred place to do a PGCE having studied French and Spanish. We had known each other a bit while we had both been students, as we had both attended St Nick's. But it was the time spent working together that started our relationship. Moving chairs, washing floors, folding service sheets are all very dull things to do, so you can chatter away about all kinds of things. We found we had so much in common. I fancied her, wanted to have sex with her, but being a good Christian boy knew that meant we had to get married first.

I first broached the subject of marriage at 11:30 on a Tuesday night, as we put away the last few chairs from an evening event of some kind. "You know, I think we should get married," were, she tells me, my exact words.

She just looked at me, and said, "I can think of more romantic locations to propose. Why don't you try again at a better time. You can finish locking up." And she left the building, leaving me to process what I'd done, and decide if I really meant it.

I did not sleep that well that Tuesday night. Open mouth, insert foot, hello insomnia and embarrassing memories, swarming like midges trying to eat me alive. But by five o'clock the following morning, after a cup of tea and a pre-dawn walk, I realised I did mean it, and so the following Thursday, suggested we went out for lunch and a walk. This time I proposed with a bit more romance; I did manage to get down on one knee, I had bought a cheap ring as a sign of my intentions, and it went far better than the not-even-dress-rehearsal of two evenings before.

Not long after we were married we were both students again. Mary doing her PGCE, me at theological college. Happily she got a job nearby, and the Diocese were kind and I got a curacy in a church close enough that she could keep that job. So when we moved to St Mark's she had worked for five years in the same school, and so it did not look too dodgy on her CV.

As I said, she knows my moods, and could sense something was wrong when she got in from work. I was sitting in my study, staring at my laptop screen, muttering to myself.

"How was your day Paul?"

I sighed. What should I say?

"You're not as happy as you were. Was this the funeral visit you did today?"

I spun round in my chair, facing her for the first time. "Yeah. They were a devoted couple. She's been completely destroyed by his death. Absolutely destroyed. It took all the wind out of my sails, like a slug ate the shoot of my hope."

"You're always so good with words."

Mary put her bag down, came into my study and sat on my lap. She stroked the top of my head and kissed it, just like she did with the kids when they were upset or grumpy about something. She gave me a hug.

I hugged back, hard. I needed to recover a vision for life, something more positive, something with some kind of hope.

Mary looked down at me. "You've not made a start on tea yet, have you?"

I shook my head.

"Well, I'm starving. Staff meeting as well as a full day teaching is good for the appetite. I only got five minutes for lunch. Wet play again. Come and be gloomy at me in the kitchen if you want."

She pecked my cheek, and got up, heading out of the room.

"I'm going to finish this, and then try and cheer up before we eat. The kids are hiding from me somewhere. I told them I was grumpy, and they took the hint." I span back round, and finished writing the story of Harold's life. Devoted husband, father and grandfather. Gone for ever, sadly missed.

What words are there to say?

I tapped away for a while. I can normally reconstruct an outline of someone's life from the conversation I have with the bereaved family. There's a fairly obvious series of questions you ask: date and place of birth, schooling, jobs, significant relationships (partner, children etc), hobbies, favourite phrases, holiday destinations, films, books, all of that sort of thing.

Sometimes there's a complicated bit, an affair, a drug habit, debts. Funerals should be honest, but not destructive. Grieving families do not always want to share all their dirty secrets with a stranger in a dog-collar. Sometimes you have to read between the silences. Happily, Harold's life was quite straightforward. He met Vera at school; they were friends, very good friends, "innocent sweethearts" was how she described it, "just holding hands occasionally" during their school days, but knowing they were meant for each other and agreeing to marry once they both had proper jobs. Harold left school at sixteen, took an apprenticeship, learnt his trade as an electrician. Vera went to secretarial school, learnt how to take shorthand, and even how to type. Once they had the jobs sorted, it was time to come together and they were married in the June after Vera's eighteenth birthday. "Eighteen years, two months, six days and a married woman. Another thing from days gone by," she had explained to me.

They had three children, all girls, all grown up and with children of their own now. Harold was interested in his grandkids, "once they were big enough to be interesting, at least. He never really did babies, but once they could walk and talk he loved spending time with them."

Apart from his gnomes, Harold had been a Red, although he had not been to a match for at least twenty years. "He said it cost too much these days. I was glad he made that choice, as we couldn't really have afforded a season ticket. We both had pensions, but they were not that generous." He was not interested in music, preferred to holiday in the UK, had no time for package tours to Spain or Turkey, but did like a dram or two of whiskey before bed, "For medicinal purposes, he always said, helped him sleep."

He was a devoted husband, faithful for sixty-one years, a good father and grandfather, who liked to teach the next generation "practical skills for real life, like how to change a plug or wire a light fitting." He did not suffer fools gladly, but would happily help you if you admitted you had made a mistake or just did not really know what to do.

And where is Harold now? That was the question that was bothering me. People talk about the dead becoming stars, or "looking down on us," but he clearly was neither a flaming ball of gas, nor an occupant of the international space station. If heaven is above us, it cannot be a physical location above our heads. Does Harold have a physical form any more? As Mrs Griffiths told it, he was not an especially religious man. I had never met him, or her, before I got the phone call booking me for the funeral. Can I speak of the resurrection hope at the funeral of a man who almost certainly did not really believe in it? If I cannot, then why are they employing me—and even if I am not personally getting paid for it, they are employing me—to take a funeral for them?

It is getting less and less common for people to turn to the Church of England when a loved one dies, which makes me think harder about those who still choose to. I mean, when people choose to do something out of the ordinary, there has to be a reason for it, and I always like to know what that reason is. Often as not, it is simply convention, a habit that has not quite died out yet. "He wasn't a religious man, but he would have wanted a vicar to take his funeral," or something paradoxical like that. But what should the vicar think when he does this? Does he believe that these people, who patently do not believe in Jesus seriously enough to actually come to church, are eternally condemned? If they are, then is it my duty to warn the surviving relatives? But going that way leads to pastoral disaster. I could not possibly introduce myself to Vera saying, "Hi, I'm Paul, I'm taking Harold's service. Did you know he's condemned to an eternity in Hell?"

So do I just ignore the fact, if it is a fact? Or do I say that I must just trust it all into the hands of Almighty God who judges everyone and will judge everyone justly? But that seems equally flawed. It seems like a cop out, refusing to take any of the responsibility that I really ought to be taking. Maybe it is simpler to be universalist, to say that God welcomes everyone to heaven, regardless of who they are or what they believe or what they've done. But in that case, where is the justice for the murderers, the rapists, the sadistic torturers of other people? And what is the point of me being a vicar?

Sometimes I can take refuge and comfort in phrases like Julian of Norwich's "All will be well, and all will be well, and all manner of things will be well." But sometimes it sounds like so much meaningless nonsense. It is not all well at the moment. Far from it. Vera is a broken wreck, her life as shattered as Marion's teacup. My hope is fading, my belief in a God who may, or may not, have called me to this role, is wavering, and I am failing to be a husband or father of any worth.

I blinked. I had been staring blankly at a computer screen for a good ten minutes. It was black, gone into power-saving mode. Maybe that was a hint. Time to stop. I woke my computer up, but only to put it properly to bed, and went out of my study to find Mary. Maybe normal life would help me leave my pit of gloom. □

Slowly climbing upward

Planning Linda Grove's funeral was an emotionally un-complicated affair. Her daughter Louise Groves, a petite brunette in her early forties, was businesslike. "Mum had a good life, the last six months of her cancer were hard, but to be honest, death is a release and we know that she had a good life."

Linda's "good life" consisted mainly of holidays, bingo, and time with her friends. She had no husband, and funded her activities from her various jobs as a cleaner, healthcare assistant and catering assistant. Nothing overly demanding, but enough to ensure there was food on the table, a roof over her head, and spending money when it was required. Louise did seem to like her mum, but was dry eyed as she talked about her, not indulging in any sentimentality or wallowing in self-pity.

I was grateful for the businesslike nature of the whole thing, especially since it would be my second funeral of the day. More to the point, I was really unsure if I could have coped with another emotionally demanding situation. There is only so much grief I can take at the moment. It is all so much simpler when people remain detached. Simpler, but my doubts wondered, perhaps less human? And there was that comment about what people would be wearing.

"Mum never liked black, so I've told them all not to wear any black. Everyone has to be in bright colours. It will be a celebration, a celebration of Mum's life."

In my head, the conversation moved on to discuss the importance of mourning, the fact that modern British society is afraid of death, and copes with this fear largely by ignoring death, storing up pastoral problems for people like me to deal with in years to come, suppressing the complex emotions of grief under a pink frock that screams "I'm in denial about Mum's death" to anyone who has ears to listen.

From my lips came, "Oh, I see. I can wear my purple funeral scarf rather than the black one if you would like?"

She looked genuinely puzzled for a moment, forehead wrinkled, pulling her head back as she thought, giving herself an extra chin in the process.

"I didn't realise there was a choice," she responded. "But if there is, then purple would be better, mainly to avoid the black, of course."

"Of course." I nodded my agreement and understanding, while in my head "Coward, coward, coward" echoed around.

The planning was almost done. I read through my notes to her, confirming I had understood everything correctly and that her chosen list of close relatives to be read out during the prayers included everyone in the appropriate order.

The whole process had taken about fifteen minutes, mainly because Louise had done a lot of preparation. She had already chosen the music for coming in and out, decided on the only hymn (All things bright and beautiful) and had jotted down some notes about her mum's life. Apparently, Linda had started to write her own eulogy, but the family had told her that was a bit over-organized, so she had settled for making sure her daughter Louise had all the key dates and people written down properly. Fifteen minutes to plan the memorial of someone's life. Not long at all, but apparently time enough.

I still had half a cup of tea to finish, and since my neck is not asbestos lined, this meant we would have to fill the time with some small talk. After a brief silence, just short enough to avoid being awkward, Louise moved first. "I really don't know how you do your job Father. I mean all that time talking about death, it must be depressing."

Ah, not small talk then. Straight for the jugular. My professional ability to lie in this particular context was fading.

"Actually yes, it can be at times."

My honesty surprised us both. I did not realise I had it in me, and she was not sure of what to say in reply. There was a brief pause, as we both assessed our conversational options. It was clearly my responsibility to get us out of the pit my trapdoor honesty had dropped us into.

"I mean, when you hear heart-wrenching stories on a regular basis, it is difficult not to be affected by them. Of course it is not as hard for me as for the close family, by any means, but dealing with death a lot of the time can be difficult. I am fortunate in having a loving wife who listens to me talk it out. Everyone needs a good listening to from time to time, and Mary does that for me."

"I like that. 'A good listening to.' I'm going to use it." She smiled, relieved that we could move on to safer territory. "I think you're right that so many problems and stresses could be solved if people took the time to listen to each other properly. I wish our boss would understand that."

"What do you do?" Yes, definitely safer ground.

As I finished my tea, I was informed of the complexities of working in insurance on the claims phone team. Apparently the issue was that everyone had to be ready to answer all calls, as well as doing the paperwork on claims, and so you might well find yourself half way through four things towards the middle of the afternoon, and end up rushing to finish. Oh, and, you're not allowed to spend time listening to people's problems when they report a theft or damage claim: get the facts down quickly and move the conversation on. It made me wonder if I was in danger of doing that sometimes when I visited a family to plan a funeral. Get the facts down and move on, quickly, make sure there is not too much pain on display or raw emotion floating around the place doing damage. All sorted in fifteen minutes. Really Paul? Or the main issues dodged one more time? Grief observed but not cared for perhaps?

As I walked back home, I replayed my conversation with Louise. "Actually yes." Maybe the sunflower of hope stood a chance after all. I was wavering between hope and despair, wanting green shoots, but expecting more slugs. Sometimes taking a funeral is just another day at the office. Other times it is an emotional roller coaster. I want to pray that God will give comfort and hope to these people, but more often than not, I leave thinking they do not even really believe he exists, let alone want to hear from him. What kind of hope am I supposed to offer, what difference can I make? Maybe John was right all along, and imagining there's no heaven is the way to go.

I asked Mary when we were tidying up the kitchen after tea. It is often the best time for a conversation with her. By bed time, I am normally far too exhausted to be coherent, especially after an evening meeting. She was telling me about the RE topic they were doing, which was rituals that mark significant parts of life.

"It used to be easier, we would just talk about christenings, weddings and a brief mention of funerals. But now most of them have not been to a christening. A wedding is a party in a hotel. And apparently I cannot talk about death too much in case I upset them. It's so annoying. I did ask them what they thought happened after death, but most had no idea. Some talked about becoming a star or 'going to heaven.' But I think it was all just words. I don't think I've ever had a class where more than one or two have had any really ideas about death."

There was a perfect opening. "I don't think I do either, anymore" I replied. "Ever since John asked me to play Imagine at the end of Marion's funeral, I have been wondering whether he wasn't right. Maybe there is nothing, that you do live, die then rot."

"Cheerful tonight, Paul." Mary looked at me, shaking her head. "Why do you beat yourself up all the time? You could get a part time job as a punch bag. Of course we all doubt some of the time. I doubt whether I'm making a difference to year four all the time, especially when its cold and raining, I've got them all day, and by 2pm everyone's climbing the walls."

I pictured her wedged up in the corner of the ceiling, shouting at her class to sit down. It was enough to stop me moaning for a moment, at least.

"You're right, I guess," I sighed. "I just need to learn to cope better. No idea how, but maybe it'll come." □

Downward?

Charles looked awful at church today. Truly awful. Like someone had died. After the service, over a cup of tea, I asked him what was wrong. I was right. Someone had died, and he never had a chance to say goodbye to them. He had told me about his brother Ezekiel. Actually I had prayed for Ezekiel's healing at least three times this past week. I always feel ever so slightly guilty about this sort of prayer, normally because I do not manage to do anything like enough of it. I promise to pray for people. I even write a list, keep it with my Bible, read it often, mentioning them to the Almighty in a sort of doctor's round kind of way. Mrs Jones, bad knee. Elisabeth, heart murmur. John, possible return of cancer. Ezekiel, something wrong with his throat. A ward list of close contacts and distant unknowns, jostling together for your attention, your faltering attempts to ask God to heal them.

Last Thursday Charles got a phone call. His brother had died. The throat problem was cancer, undiagnosed, untreated, a gigantic tumour which choked the life out of him.

"The message was that 'Ezekiel's funeral was tomorrow.'" Charles explained to me.

I was confused by the tenses of that sentence. "Was tomorrow?" My wrinkled forehead sought clarification. We were standing just past the serving hatch, in danger of causing a traffic jam, blocking access to the budget biscuits. As we walked to find a better, more private, space, Charles explained.

"Yeah, it was on Friday. That's normal in Uganda. No way to preserve the body, likelihood of disease. Best get it in the ground as soon as. Dead today, buried tomorrow, or the day after at the latest. What else can you do?" He gestured in despair.

So Charles had no chance to go to his own brother's funeral. He ran up a hefty phone bill listening in to a big chunk of the service on his sister's mobile. Said his own prayers as if by the grave. He hopes to go in the New Year, when the weather is drier. He will visit the grave then, and that will have to be enough.

I asked him what a Ugandan funeral was like, and it was fascinating. There were some elements I recognised, the standard things you might expect. But there were many others I did not. For starters, it was not in the church. It was in Ezekiel's village, everyone gathering in a central location, and taking it in turns to share memories or to speak of the Christian hope. When he said village, Charles explained, he meant a few mud huts really, not a village like I might imagine one.

"Everyone gathers. Everyone drops everything and just comes to the funeral. There might be seven or eight hundred people at a big funeral, and even for Ezekiel, I was told it was over four hundred."

I was surprised at the numbers, and even more surprised to discover that Charles now had to foot his share of the bill for feeding them all. "I will pay when I visit. It will probably be a bit over one hundred pounds. Not enough to make it worth sending by transfer. The fees are too high."

I tried to imagine this scene, of hundreds of people, all sitting on chairs or in the dirt, eating rice and beans and a bit of meat, all in honour of a man they may have known, or maybe had just heard about. Apparently it is a standard part of saying goodbye, of paying your respects. "It is a matter of honour to have a big funeral, even if you cannot afford it. As the rich man who has gone to the West, it is my duty to pay."

Charles smiled wryly. His café did turn a modest profit, but mainly because he worked all hours, took very few holidays and had built a reputation as a supplier of quality business lunches as well as giving people on their lunch breaks or shopping coffee breaks good service at reasonable prices. "For the UK, I am poor, but for Uganda, I am a wealthy man. He was my brother. I will pay."

If I let him, the Weasel would enjoy chewing on all of this. Sudden death, unable to say goodbye, but expected to foot the bill. Where is the justice in that, he wants to know. Where is the unfailing mercy of God? He is right of course. I have no answers, only an awkward hand on the arm and offer of prayer to Charles.

What do you do in these circumstances? What comfort can you offer? Funerals, much as I hate them, at least offer a chance to say goodbye. Without even that, the black hole is just bigger, easier to fall into. I talked a bit more with Charles, and we agreed that I would go and see him on Monday evening, to hold a short service together with his family, to give him some kind of closure.

As Charles walked off, Caroline, who had been hovering in a "I want to ask you something" holding pattern swooped in. "Paul, are you free sometime this week? I'd like to ask you something."

"Sure, let's fix a time."

I was lost in thought as I walked home after locking up twenty minutes later. I'm trying to water my sunflower, trying not to think of my doubts as a wriggling animal controlling my mind. For some reason the Almighty seems to think the best way of this happening is for me to be constantly surrounded by death. It reminds me of the warning my old boss used to give: only pray for patience if you're ready for God to surround you with annoying people that test your patience. Only pray to grow in love if you're ready to be surrounded by idiots who are hard to love. And so on. Only point out to God that you're a vicar who cannot really cope with death and funerals if you want your mind to be filled with them all of the time.

"So here's the thing," I announced to the family over our traditional Sunday lunch of pizza, "I think I have made a mistake."

"Only one Dad?" Jack smiled.

"Yeah, Dad, you're bound to have made more than one," Annabelle supported her brother.

I glanced at Mary, hoping for support, but all I got was, "What mistake are you thinking of in particular?"

Three against one. Was it going to get better or worse? Worse.

"Well, have you heard what happened to Charles' brother?"

They had not, so I explained as best I could. In my view Annabelle is eleven, a vicar's daughter who sees enough of the mess of normal human life that a bit more will make no real difference. Jack started speculating what would have happened to Ezekiel's body if they had not buried him so quickly, but a firmly raised maternal eyebrow and a "Jack, not at the table," soon ended that line of investigation.

Then Annabelle remembered. "But how is that your mistake Dad?" A scratch of the head to show her confusion. A deft move to get the last slice of Hawaiian while I framed my reply.

"No, no, that wasn't the mistake." I took off my glasses and rubbed my hand across my eyes as I tried to marshall my thoughts. "Its about death generally. Its getting me down. The mistake was telling God about it, as now I seem to be surrounded by death even more than normal."

"Oh, okay, I get you." Jack claimed. His sister clearly did not. She just looked at me. So did Mary, with 'was that really a helpful comment?' floating just above her raised eyebrows, silently rebuking my new-found honesty.

I decided to try and prove why I was being helpful.

"Well, think about Nanny Margaret."

That warning sign above Mary's head got bigger, lit up in neon and now came with "Caution. Hazard ahead" in even bigger letters.

"Yeah, Nanny Margaret," I plunged on, in the white-water rapids now, my best hope to keep us moving through the water to calm on the other side. "I've found it hard getting over her death, as I know you guys have as well. And it has made doing funerals for other people harder as well. I made the mistake of telling God about it and suggesting he might help me deal with it. His response has been for me to get loads more funerals, which I am finding hard going. But I am learning that I have to be honest about my feelings. And I think if I cannot be honest with you guys, who can I be honest with? I'm sorry that this is painful, but maybe if we talk about our pain, we can learn to carry it more easily."

"I miss Nanny Margaret too Dad," Annabelle said. "She was always such good fun. She used to read me stories all the time, and she had some cool old dolls. I loved them when I was little."

"Yeah, and her puddings were the best. Her treacle tart was so much nicer than Mum's." Jack offered, taking the last two pieces of Pepperoni Extra Hot, leaving me with salad if I wanted any more to eat.

"It was." Mary surprised Jack by not raising to his bait. Culinary prowess may be a badge of honour for her, but some things are more important. "I think your dad has been brave in telling us what's been getting him down. Now we know why he's been so grumpy recently."

"I'm sorry about that as well." I rubbed my hands together and offered compensation: "Who wants an ice cream? The van's bound to come past sometime soon."

Everyone wanted an ice cream, especially one from the van. I had already treated them all to a cake yesterday, and now an ice cream today. I needed a better strategy for apology that unhealthy food. But "I'm sorry I upset you, here, have this banana by way of apology," is not really the most effective of strategies. Just saying sorry should be enough, but I kind of want to do something to show that I mean it.

Family are important, and if I do get the chance to talk to older people about the regrets that swarm around them like flies, then too much time at work and consequently ignoring the family are often mentioned, especially by men. I find myself doing the self-same thing. I know I should not, I know I ought to spend more time with them, but somehow I cannot help it. Work takes over, other people's problems become more interesting—or perhaps less painful—than your own, and before I know it, the week has gone by, I have been out too much and opportunities for family time are lost.

Charles' story made me think about my own family. Since Mum died, I rarely talk to Susan. Two years younger, but a world away. Another thing to make more effort for, perhaps another part of why I am finding life so hard at the moment. If we are not connected to those we love, perhaps we stop being who we really are? □

Mondays

The problem with a Sunday is that the next day is a Monday. This chronological conundrum is shared by many people, invariably those for whom Sunday is the last day of their weekend and Monday the first of their working week. This is not my reason for disliking Mondays. Sunday and Monday are both working days. My "weekend' is often a Friday or a Saturday, but occasionally just fiction, mainly because of my inability to say no. So all in all, I do not especially mind some Mondays. But those Mondays that end with a church council meeting are in the "less than decent" part of the calendar.

We obviously have to have a church council. We clearly have to make decisions about complex matters related to church life. We have a duty to ensure the accounts are properly presented, and that the church remains financially solvent. The problem is that doing all these things is quite difficult when your congregation is, in the main, fairly elderly, just about surviving on modest pensions, not especially interested in due process and in denial about the fairly obvious fact that before too long there will be fewer people, less money and eventually so few people attending any activity that the church does that closure is inevitable.

Just when I was starting to feel a bit more positive about the death of individuals who are my pastoral responsibility, I realised that I also had to think about the death of the church of which I was the minister. No one really wants to be the one who says the final final blessing, who does the last ever service in a particular church, but for many churches it has to happen sometime. Take St Nathaniel's. Richard Hobson arrived to a complete mess, with only a handful of people attending. He somehow turned it around and in its heyday, St Nathaniel's was a powerhouse. Apparently at its busiest three thousand attended on a Sunday. Now, over a century later, there is nothing at all. No vicar, no congregation, nothing. St Mark's did not have thousands attending, although there were those who remembered days when more than a hundred were in regular attendance. Now, we averaged forty. A decent enough crowd, but not exactly earth shattering, given there were about seven and a half thousand in the parish.

For reasons that seemed sensible at the time, and now seemed like utter idiocy, I had decided it would be a good idea to talk about these issues in our PCC meeting. It was not the best meeting I have ever chaired. I would be so much better at chairing meetings if there were no other people there, or at least if all the other people there agreed with me over most of the difficult items we had to discuss. I guess that makes me a bit like the librarians who moan that their book would be so much better cared for if people stopped borrowing them to read them, or the university administrators who wish for a quieter life with no actual students actually studying anything. But such is the refuge of the slightly incompetent, a band whose ranks I have quite happily joined.

At least the earlier part of the evening had gone well. I had been to see Charles on my way over to church. I had brought with me a basic order of service for a funeral. Over a cup of tea, we talked about Ezekiel. He was four years younger than Charles. Not that gifted academically, more interested in working the land than in anything else. While Charles was ambitious, wanted to see the world, had jumped at a chance to get a visa to come to the UK, Ezekiel was not bothered in the slightest.

He had just concentrated on growing sogum and a few other crops. He kept three cows, made more than enough money to be comfortable, but not so much that other people noticed him and started taking any from him. All Ezekiel's nine children had completed primary school by the time he became ill, so his family were way ahead of most of their contemporaries. Charles makes sure they have always got mosquito nets, which means they have all made it through early childhood, and now have a decent chance of surviving as adults. Until that conversation, I had not really appreciated the fragility of life in rural Uganda. Death is common there. Everyone was sad that Ezekiel died, but no one was surprised. Living till you are fifty is the exception, not the norm, apparently.

Once we had finished talked, I said a few prayers, and Charles also prayed, thanking God for his brother and asking forgiveness for not going to the funeral. I found the second prayer odd, as I thought it was entirely reasonable that Charles had not gone. But Charles was still hovering between remorse and realism, and it was not my place to tell him where he should stand.

A few more minutes chatting, and then I had to go. Time to make sure the chairs and tables were all out for the church council meeting. Time to enter that alternative reality that is a committee meeting.

Is it something about sitting around four tables arranged in a square that turns normally rational and reasonable human beings into complete pains? Is it because Christians think we have to be nice that we tolerate people who object to everything that is brought to us to consider? It always amazes me that I can have lovely conversations with all of our church council when I see them in their homes or on a Sunday, but put us around a table and we seem to argue and procrastinate about the most simple of things.

That particular meeting was not too bad. We dispatched with the mundane business items, about rubber stamping the decisions about things such as where the proceeds from the Lent Lunches would go, and whether the fledgling youth group could buy a second cheap sofa, so they did not have to try and cram five teenagers onto one two-seater, something the leaders and girls were keener to avoid that one of the boys. Happily Jack was in favour of the second sofa, especially if he got to with me to IKEA to buy it, as Swedish meatballs are a favourite of his. Even getting through these items took us longer than I thought it would; thirty minutes of meeting dealt with, and nothing controversial so far. The colour of the sofa was part of the problem, but happily the fact that it was removable and washable was met with approval by all.

Then we had to decide about a more complicated item. What was the long-term mission strategy of the church? Did we have any plans to keep going? How were we going to manage it?

One view was the "run a course and convert the parish" strategy. We do run explorer courses twice a year, offering people a chance to find out about what it means to be a Christian. One in September and one in January. I used to think we should do a third one in the summer, but no one was interested, so after a few years of sitting around in the church on a Wednesday night like Billy-no-mates, I stopped bothering. Each time we run some kind of a course, two or three, or occasionally as many as five people gather. Normally one is from church, after a refresher, or wanting to ensure the vicar is not lonely. Sometimes the other people stay, other times they conclude Christianity is not for them. Our growth rate through running these courses is more than offset by the rate at which people are dying or moving away, I pointed out. We needed something more.

Another view was the "we've got a youth group, so we'll be fine." It is true that there are actually teenagers in St Marks. Two happen to be the vicar's kids, but they are still genuine teenagers (ish). There are three others, also children of committed members. The youth enjoy their own sessions, largely loath what happens on a Sunday morning, and so perhaps, I gently ventured, should not be considered the mainstay of a plan for the future of St Marks.

This nay-saying was not winning me any friends, but I was enjoying the catharsis of honesty, and decided I would deal with the consequences at a later date.

My personal favourite of a suggestion came next: the new noticeboard. Apparently, once we repainted our noticeboard, with the morning service time in bigger letters, people would flood in. I'm all for publicity, but informed everyone I "remained unsure" that this was the solution to all our concerns. Worth doing, I suppose, subject to cost. Tony offered to find us a price, and we agreed to think about it at the next meeting.

It had taken us an hour and forty minutes to get this far with the meeting, and the noticeboard had somehow managed to require a twenty minute discussion, including a short monologue about the best type of font for catching the attention of passers-by. With the time heading for nine o'clock, I decided that maybe we would have to carry this discussion over to another meeting. "Maybe," I proposed, "We need to not just think of ways of getting people to come into the church, but also ways in which we could go out into the community to engage with them. Can you take five minutes to come up with ideas in pairs please?"

People were clearly tired by this point. Most people did not really have much of an idea, although the possibility of offering to "do old people's gardens" from seventy-one year old Richard did make me smile. "Let's have a chat about that afterwards Richard, great idea."

Where there's life, there's hope, apparently. So if there are not many signs of life, is it foolish for me to still try and cling on to some kind of hope? □

Remembering Bruce

"And here's Bruce. He's always close to my heart."

I have to say that as a minister, I am always concerned when any woman I'm visiting starts to unbutton her blouse at any point during a pastoral visit. Even if the woman in question is in her late fifties and I do not find her in the slightest bit attractive. Sometimes you find yourself wishing it were possible to vanish, and here I was wishing this comfy arm chair would swallow me whole.

The week had been largely uneventful. I spent some time preparing for the following Sunday, quite a bit of time making sure I had the details of Harold's funeral and Linda's funeral organized, and more time than I wanted dealing with emails, paperwork and the like. I did manage to see a few other people during the week, and maintained a relatively positive frame of mind right up until Friday morning.

I surprised myself with what happened on Friday. I managed to keep the two services completely separate. Harold's was first, and the harder of the two. Vera held her composure. I think she had done most of her crying in the days before the funeral. A few tiny streams of tears escaped, but not the flood I had wondered might come. They brought a gnome with them, perched it on the coffin during the service. It transformed things, made it both a solemn and a happy affair. They asked me if I wanted it after the service, but I declined. My suggestion of giving them away had been taken up, and the service sheet included an invitation to "pop round to see Vera in the coming weeks, and take one of Harold's gnomes with you." A stroke of genius, I realised, as even if only a few of the hundred or so mourners did decide to take up the offer, it would mean Vera was not so isolated as I feared she might be. Even after he'd died, Harold's gnomes were bringing life. The family did not stay long. They left virtually straight away to go to a hotel somewhere by Sefton Park, for sandwiches and memories.

Linda's funeral was simple. Although the clothes were brighter than the black of Harold's, the service itself was perhaps slightly less cheerful. Much smaller, with a couple of what looked like hospice nurses sitting at the back. They often do, if a patient has been with them for a while. Maybe it is part of how they cope with a job that means they see far more death than most of us. Or perhaps it is a sign of respect for the family. I have never really asked. Linda's family lingered, kind of like they had not quite said goodbye.

I refused to listen to my doubts. Yes, it was tragic to see what Harold's death had done to Vera, but it was not up to me to bring her the hope she needed. Yes, it was sad that Louise had lost her mum, and sad that she was hiding her grief behind her colourful clothes. But if she said nothing to me about it, then I could do nothing to help her.

After the two services, I took a longer than usual lunch break, reading the whole of the paper with a second, and indeed a third, cup of tea. Friday afternoon was not the time for sitting in the office, and when Caroline had asked me to come and see her on Sunday, I had booked in the visit for this afternoon.

But now I found myself sitting opposite a middle-aged woman who appeared to be about to take her clothes off. I really did not understand what was going on. I had come to visit Caroline, Mrs Caroline Short, who had been attending St Mark's for a few weeks now. I never like to rush in to see people too soon, I think it comes across overly keen and a bit too intense. After a month of regular attendance, it is acceptable to ask if it is alright to pop round for a cup of tea and a chat, although of course in this case, she had got in first. I had been hoping to avoid the subject of death. It has been far too much on my mind lately, and had involved too much of that particular day. But of course Caroline is a widow, a relatively recently widow, her husband having died only a year ago. Her daughter lives near us, and she'd move to be closer to family now she was all alone. Well, alone, except for carrying her husband's ashes in a diamond pendant around her neck.

"Sorry, all of your husband's ashes are in that necklace?" Stay focused man, stay focused, ignore the unbuttoned blouse, ignore the peeping bra strap, winking suggestively at you. Focus on the pastoral encounter. You should get out of this fine, but concentrate on your job.

"Yes all of him!" She laughed, throwing her head back, exposing her long neck.

"Yes," she said, stowing Bruce safely out of the way, and happily buttoning him back out of sight. "Close to my heart. I knew I wasn't going to stay in Derby, so I brought him with me. Didn't want to leave him alone up there."

In an idle moment waiting to see a member of staff or a grieving family at the local Coop undertakers I have often looked at the leaflet advertising the facility of turning cremation ashes into diamonds. I suppose it is just a very expensive transition from one form of carbon to another. I have often wondered who, if anyone, uses these services. Rich widows I thought, and it seems I was right.

Actually I have no idea whether Mrs Short—do call me Caroline dear—is wealthy or not. Given she lives in our neighbourhood, I would guess she is not exactly super-rich. Comfortable perhaps, in her flat, closer to her daughter, but with a fifteen-minute buffer zone meaning they were unlikely to bump into each other too often.

Wealth, and a willingness to part with at least some of it so that St Mark's can keep functioning would be a welcome bonus. Regular attendance at services was a wonderful first step. An ability to ask out-of-the-blue questions an added advantage.

"So Paul, you don't mind me calling you Paul do you?"

"That's fine." It was her house, her chocolate biscuits.

"So Paul, I wanted to ask you about Lent courses. You do run Lent courses at St Mark's don't you?"

"Yes we do. Lent starts in a fortnight, as you probably know."

A nod.

Time for the embarrassing bit.

"But I'm not one hundred percent sure exactly what we will be studying yet."

"Meaning you have no real idea because you've been too busy with other things?" She smiled. There was no barb in the question, just blunt honesty. A smile that told me to call a spade a spade please, not a soil relocation system.

Bluff called, it was time to come clean. "Yes, something like that. I need to make a firm plan this week, if I'm being honest, and have been looking at some courses, but none has really grabbed me. I should probably make a final decision on Saturday morning. Most likely we will use the Church Urban Fund one. That's what I did last year, and it was quite good. Folks told me they enjoyed it."

"Oh good. Does that mean I can put in a request?"

This was new. Someone making a request for a Lent group topic. Normally the challenge was in persuading people to actually turn up. The sessions had been advertised as being on a Tuesday night for at least a month now, and as far as I knew, only two people had signed up. Maybe people were waiting to know what the course was. At least, that was Mary's view. "You need to tell people more dear. Then they'll sign up." But it seemed Caroline was willing to sign up regardless, so maybe I would win this argument with my wife.

"Can we talk about death?" Caroline asked.

"Sorry?" I was still a bit dazed by the bra-strap earlier, currently slightly lost in thinking about who, if anyone, else might be coming to the Lent group, and whether I would prove Mary wrong. I certainly had not seen this one coming.

"About death and bereavement and what the Bible says. I really have no idea, and I need to talk to someone. It seemed like a suitable time really, the run up to Easter, to talk about death, don't you think?"

Actually, I did think. I thought lots of things. That many people would hate this topic. That maybe I would enjoy it. That I wanted to ask John to come, although he would almost certainly say no. That Charles might possibly be up for it. That I would end up running two groups on two nights, but that maybe it would be worth it.

"Well, actually, that does make sense," I ventured. "I don't think it would be everyone's cup of tea, and that would probably mean I would end up running two groups on two separate nights."

"Oh no," she interrupted. "I thought we could just have an chat for an hour or so before the Lent Lunches. Talking about death and then coming home to an empty house and a cold bed. No thanks."

She had a point. And a plan it seemed. Best to do what she said. □

First Meeting

"Yes, I know Mrs Lucas will have to join us. I know that her brother recently died. In fact, I was talking to her about the plan just before the service started today, and she said she thought it would be wonderful. Apparently she has been thinking a bit about Frankie's death and would be quite pleased of the chance to talk a bit more."

Joan was silenced for a moment. She had come to find me straight after the service, to voice her list of objections to the vicar's hair brained scheme for having a discussion group about death just before the Lent Lunches on a Thursday. So far we had tackled the fact that the Bible could be read in a discussion group, but it would not be a straight Bible study; that the meeting would take place in the youth lounge, so no one would be under her feet as she set up the main hall for lunch; that the vicar would indeed perform his Lenten duty of setting up the tables and chairs; and that we would begin the lunch with a brief Agape communion. Having failed to bust the vicar so far, Joan had played her trump card, Mrs Lucas.

Why no one called Doreen by her first name I was never entirely clear. Face-to-face, I always did, as she had told me to the first time I met her. But when anyone spoke about her, it was always Doreen Lucas, or more likely, Mrs Lucas. She was seventy-three, a life long spinster, who until a year ago had been the main carer for her disabled younger brother. Physically, Frankie was fine. But mentally there was something wrong—I never learnt the technical diagnosis. I had always found him friendly, but slow to do anything, and only able to manage very simple tasks. His conversation was limited, although he was always sure to tell you whether Liverpool had won or lost if there had been a match the day before. He had died aged seventy. "He made his three score and ten," as Doreen put it.

I never heard Doreen complain or grumble about her lot in life. She had worked until she was sixty, as a doctor's receptionist. During her working life, her free time was taken up with a combination of caring for her brother, running the family home and coming to church on a Sunday and for the midweek Bible study. On retirement, these part-time activities became full-time ones. She took Frankie out to a day centre once or twice a week, brought him to church for the Sunday service and the lunch club on a Thursday, and they went all sorts of places on the bus. He also retired at fifty-eight, from his job in the local Coop, where he had kept the shelves neat and tidy, but had never been allowed near a till.

Since Frankie's death, Doreen had managed to get out and about a bit more. She had never owned a car, never learnt to drive, but would walk or stand and wait for a bus, or gratefully accept a lift if one was offered. She loved being with other people, and I had no doubts about her joining my little band. Joan always gave Doreen a lift to church for Lent Lunches, and because Joan was chief cook, that meant Doreen got there at 10:30, but she was a bit too frail to help in the kitchen, so oftentimes she just sat in the youth lounge and read her paper.

So far, it was going to be Doreen, Caroline and myself, meeting in the youth lounge at eleven am for about an hour. We had to be in the main hall in time for me to do the informal communion at 12:30, so there was a clear end point if things got a bit complicated. I gave an open invitation during the notices in the Sunday service, but did not get much positive take up. Charles told me that I should do it in the evening, and I explained that Caroline had specifically asked for daytime. I promised him that I would at least go and talk with him again. That seemed to be enough for him.

That Tuesday, I called in on John, just to see how he was feeling now Marion's funeral had happened and he was getting used to his "new normal" as I like to call it. I told him about the group, more as a means of making conversation than with any expectation he would be interested, but he said he was. He had given up working full time to care for Marion, and although he was starting to get bits of work—there's always plenty for an electrician to do if he wants to—there was no immediate rush to being overly busy. "I can certainly have an early lunch on a Thursday for a few weeks. Probably do me good to talk." I also rang Vera, but she said she was fine. Most of the other funerals I had done recently were not at all church related, so I did not bother ringing anyone else.

John, Caroline, Doreen and me. What a collection of people. I began to hope that no one else would join us. I felt I could be honest with those three, and that we might all be able to help each other somehow.

No one else did join us that first week.

I got there at 10:30 and tidied up the mess left by the teenagers while Doreen sat and chatted with me about nothing in particular.

Caroline arrived at 10:45, with a box of biscuits. "I know there's lunch next and I know its Lent, but I felt a discussion like this needed decent biscuits, and anyway, a friend gave these to me and if I leave them at home I will eat them all and get fat." she explained in one breath.

"Chocolate biscuits are always fine by me."

John was five minutes early. "Thought I'd beat the rush" he explained. "My van's in the car park. That's fine isn't it? Parked out the way in the corner, didn't want to make the grannies walk too far for their lunch."

"That's fine John. Cuppa? Caroline's brought us some biscuits."

Everyone settled and I began by explaining the ground rules: no question to stupid; everything said in this room stayed in this room; questions to people had to be about facts, and no one was allowed to offer unsolicited advice on how someone else should cope with bereavement.

"We're all different, we all handle death differently," I concluded my opening speech. "I thought we'd begin," I went on, taking silence for assent, "by introducing ourselves and talking a bit about why we're here and what we're hoping for in the next few weeks. I'll begin. I'm Paul, I'm the vicar. I'm partly here because Caroline asked me if we could run these sessions. But I'm partly here because I'm not quite sure what I think about death and what happens next. I used to be completely sure, but since my Mum died, its got harder to have black-and-white certainty, and I think it would do me good to talk a bit more about it."

Watching their faces, I decided that was enough for now. I gestured with both hands, an open invitation. "There's no set order; who would like to go next?"

"I'm Doreen. I think I know what happens when you die. You go to be with Jesus. Where that is and how it works I have no idea. But I believe my Frankie is there. Oh, and before you make the mistake people often made, Frankie was my brother, not my husband." She smiled, used to that misunderstanding.

"I'm John. I'm not a Christian, but I think you all know my wife Marion was. She died of cancer quite recently. I think I've come here because Paul let us have Imagine at the end of Marion's funeral. When he introduced the song, he said 'Imagine there's no heaven, its easy if you try. For John that is all too easy. For Marion, next to impossible. I do not know where any of you stand. Maybe closer to John, or maybe closer to Marion. The thing I have learnt from both of them is the importance of being honest about what we believe, and staying in close relationship even when we profoundly disagree.' I'm wondering how close this John stands to the John that Paul mentioned. Maybe not a close as you think Paul."

"I'm Caroline. My husband Bruce died a wee while ago, but I still have him with me, on my necklace. Maybe one week I'll tell you the story of why." Happily Caroline was wearing the diamond on display above her jumper this week. "I am here because I think it is time I began to think a bit more about death, and decide exactly what I think about it."

There was a stillness in the room, a reverent quality that I had not felt in a long time, of people being respectful as others shared just as much of themselves as they felt able to for that moment. Opening a Bible felt like a crashing gear change, a wrong move. We were all a bit like turtles that had crawled out of their shells for a look around. Too much light or heat would burn us. Best to keep things gentle.

"Why don't we talk a bit more about those whom we've loved who have died?" I offered.

"Sounds good to me," agreed John.

The ladies nodded their assent.

"Can you tell us some more about your Mum, Paul? Why was that so hard?"

I looked at John. I was not used to being the one who had to answer the hard questions. But there was absolutely no reason why I should not, and maybe going first would be for the best.

I talked for a bit about the pain of watching someone you love slowly leave while their physical body is still there. The challenge of not knowing if the three hours in the car for an hour with someone would be worth it. Somehow I digressed into the silly things, like the smell of boiled cabbage that pervaded the nursing home, and discovered that Doreen had similar views about the institution that Frankie had spent his final years in, and that Caroline thought there was similar smell in the hospital ward where her Bruce had spent his last three weeks. John said he was just glad Marion died at home, in a house that smelt of his socks.

I talked some more about my Mum. The times when she had screeched with rage at me, sworn at me using words I had not realised she even knew. The times of confusion and terror, especially just after she moved into the home, when she would wake up with no real idea of where she was, or indeed who she was. The slow descent into silence. The fact that I was not sure whether it was worse being sworn at or having one-sided conversations with the mute shrivelled yet still breathing woman who used to be my mother. I had not talked about all these things for a long time. They floated into the room, balloons of grief and regret, gathering near the ceiling. Gathering to be left behind.

In the next thirty minutes I heard many stories that I had heard before, or even been part of, because I had been quite involved with both Frankie and Marion's last few months and weeks of life. I learnt about Bruce, who I had never met. A hernia that went untreated and became septic, leading to blood poisoning. An illness not spotted by a locum GP who did a house call on a Friday, and the damage was irreversible by the Monday when the regular GP visited and sent him straight to hospital. He died three weeks later. Caroline visited him every day, but he never really talked to her. Doreen had visited Frankie every day for two years, three months and fourteen days. This was not said as a boast, but a simple answer to an innocent question. "It was my new job. Got it a few years after retirement. Kept me out of mischief." I could not imagine Doreen in mischief.

That revelation led to a discussion of bus routes, standing in the snow waiting for a bus that does not turn up and why the church had not done more to help Doreen. "Oh, it was not a problem. Fresh air does you good," was her firm response. John remained unconvinced. I remained guilty.

I think it was the refreshing honesty combined with the lack of an agenda or destination that I enjoyed most of that all too-short hour. I called us to order after an hour, to wrap things up.

"We've talked about a lot today. Let's have a moment of quiet where we can pray if we want to."

After some silence, I said, "Father, thank you that you've been with us, and thank you for helping us talk about death. Please help us to keep talking and to understand a bit better and a bit more. Amen."

We agreed that for the next week, I would find one or two Bible passages for us to talk about. John said he might want to disagree with them, and we all agreed that was fine. Then it was time to go for lunch. □

Second Meeting

It was an interesting week. I had another funeral on the Monday. It was not the easiest: the guy had died from liver problems, which is normally all the family will say when the real cause is alcohol poisoning. He was only thirty-four. According to his mum he was single, but a lady approached me as we left the crem, thanked me for doing such a lovely service and introduced herself as Terry's girlfriend. I did a double take, apologising profusely for not mentioning her. I explained that it was because I was not aware of her existence.

"No worries mate, I knew they wouldn't tell you about me. Even though we'd been together four years, we weren't married or anything. I think they'll be glad to see the last of me."

All I felt was sympathy for her, anger at the fact that she was missed out of Terry's life story and a sadness that the world is this messed up. There was no hint of the black gloom about the heartlessness of the world that I thought

I might have experienced. Like the Weasel was having a holiday maybe. Or that he knew I was going to talk back at him, so he was bidding his time. Maybe this talking about death was a good idea, after all.

The other Lent Group, however, was depressing me a bit. There were only eleven of us, and two of them were myself and Doreen, both from the "death group" as we seemed to be known. That meant only nine new people doing a Lent group, under a quarter of the regular congregation. We were talking about Jesus sending out his followers to go do miracles: heal the sick, raise the dead, preach the good news. The notes encouraged us to discuss what we could do in our community: have a concert to raise money for church funds, have a stall at the community fair (in aid of church funds) or maybe run a holiday club at Easter (but charge, so it does not impact church funds). I think I preferred Richard's idea of doing gardening for old folks. Sometimes even my hardest is nowhere near good enough.

Even though there were only going to be four of us the following Thursday, it somehow felt more worthwhile than the eleven on a Tuesday night.

"I thought maybe we could talk a bit about Lazarus today," I began, once everyone had a drink and they had all claimed the same spot on the two sofas. I always prefer a chair when I'm leading a group. Means I do not accidentally put my arm around a parishioner when I get carried away with the conversation.

"Who's he then?" John wanted to know.

"Short version: mate of Jesus' who dies and who Jesus brings back to life. Long version is here in John II." I explained as I handed out Bibles. "It's marked in all of them. I haven't prepared lots to say, you'll be pleased to hear, so I thought we'd just read it through and then each say what struck us about the story. I'll read it all, and you concentrate on listening, if that's okay?"

I read it through. The Lazarus story always makes me think, and it made them think too.

"What's always struck me," Doreen offered when I invited their reflections, "is how Jesus waits before he goes to Martha and Mary. Like he is making completely sure their brother is good and dead before he turns up. It's this mix of compassion and heartlessness, I think."

"Compassion and heartlessness?" Caroline tilted her head to the left quizzically.

"Yes, well, it was obviously compassion for Martha and Mary—and Lazarus I guess—that meant Jesus raised him. But it was kind of heartless to let him die, when he possibly could have hurried there and healed him this side of death's door, as it were, rather than calling him back out."

"But this Lazarus, guy, he's dead, right?" John needed clarification. "I mean, I thought Christians believed that after the resurrection no one was dead. I'm sure that's what Marion used to say."

"Yes, he died. There are a few stories of Jesus having power over death, and you even hear about it occasionally today, but the people always die again. So this isn't the final resurrection, if that's what you mean."

105

"Sorry, people get raised from the dead today, I mean, not with CPR or whatever, actual dead people actually alive again. Really?" John's scepticism was clear from both his tone of voice and body language.

"So I've heard Christians claim. So the Bible stories say. Some people say it still happens today. I try to keep an open mind. I mean, if it happened before, then I guess it could happen again." Caroline said.

John still looked a bit unsure, but he didn't voice an objection, so she took it as permission to continue. "My question is about how upset Jesus gets about death. I mean, preachers sometimes make a big thing of 'shortest verse in the Bible, just two words, Jesus wept.' Now, aside from the fact that John never wrote in chapter and verse, so it's a bit of a silly comment, what does it mean that Jesus wept at Lazarus' grave? Was it because he was sad Lazarus had died? That kind of doesn't work, because he knew he would raise him. Was he sad because no one believed in him? That also kind of doesn't work, because he knew people would reject him. Maybe split the difference? A bit of both?"

The three of them looked at me, expectantly.

I shrugged, palms upwards in ignorance. "Really not sure. Let's try and picture the scene, see what makes sense. Jesus has already spoken with both Martha and Mary, they have all gone to the tomb where Lazarus has been buried for four days, tradition would dictate that Jesus should mourn at the tomb. Mourning would obviously include crying. But he's not always one for following tradition, so maybe there's another reason as well. I think probably tears because of the power of death and the destruction it brings, but also tears of anger and frustration that people do not believe, although I don't want to make Jesus sound like an angry toddler. I think Caroline's suggestion is as good as any."

"If Jesus cries because his friend has died, then we should cry at funerals as well," offered Doreen.

"I'm not quite sure if that is what this is all about, but I certainly agree with the idea. Crying at a funeral ought to be encouraged, in my view" I replied.

That was the first of a number of tangents as we meandered around the Bible passage. We all agreed that crying at funerals was good, although John wanted a caveat, that the tears had to be genuine, not theatrical wailing or crocodile tears. He added that personally a private moment in the loo before the crem was more his style. Caroline agreed, saying that she had done exactly the same thing. We also wondered about how helpful it was to actually view the deceased at any point prior to the funeral. None of them were especially keen on having a viewing at home the day before the funeral, which surprised me slightly, because such things are quite common in Liverpool. Mind you, the story I told may have unduly influenced them.

I cannot remember the lady's name any more. I think it may have been Sheila, but I am probably making it up. Anyway, she was brought home and laid in state in the front room. The family duly gathered for the viewing, and for food and beers in her memory. I came, gathered them around the open coffin, said a few prayers, blessed the St Christopher necklace her nephew gave me and tied it around her cold neck. I stayed for a cup of tea and a cake. The family settled in for a few hours drinking in her memory.

Eventually everyone except Sheila's daughter went home. Said daughter was heading for bed when out of the front room she heard an eerie "Hello? Hello? Helloooo?" As far as she knew there was no one else alive in the house, and panicking that her mum may be stuck in the coffin she rang her brother to ask him to come over quick. He answered on the second ring and before she could say a word, he said, "Oh, have you found our Stella's mobile then?" This slightly took her by surprise, but a few minutes later all was clear.

Stella's ring tone was "Hello, Hello, Hellooo" and the phone had been plugged in to charge and forgotten in the living room. I think the poor girl had to come and sleep in Nan's house as punishment for scaring her aunt Sheila. Zombie phones are better than zombie grannies, but even so.

The question we kept coming back to, though, was exactly what to make of what Jesus did for Lazarus. We all agreed that—provided it actually happened and was not, as John put it, "some kid's story" then it was clearly a staggeringly impressive thing to have happened. But the fact of the matter is that, at the end of the day, Lazarus still died. We wondered for a while whether he might actually have been a bit miffed that Jesus had brought him back to life, in the sense that eternity with God had to be better than this earth. But, as Doreen pointed out, his sisters needed him, and he was bound to be concerned for their well being as well as his own happiness, so he could not have been miffed for long.

John put his finger on the problem: "I know Jesus says that he is the 'resurrection and the life' in this story, but what he did for Lazarus, that's not a real resurrection, is it? Resurrection is when you live, die, live again and don't die again. What happened to Lazarus was like delayed action CPR. Impressive, granted, not something they'd do on Casualty or House or any of them programs. But not what kept Marion so cheerful in the face of death. She wasn't looking forward to coming back to see me again, I don't think. I know she wanted me to join her, but I remain unconvinced about this whole God business, and I think maybe this resurrection stuff is right at the centre of it. Time's getting on now, and I need to shoot to go sort a lady's cooker out before her kids get back wanting their tea. But maybe next time we can talk more about the resurrection please?"

Liturgical tradition would suggest that talking about Jesus' resurrection too much in Lent is a bit like opening your birthday presents a month early, only on a much grander scale. But requests like "please can I talk to you about Jesus' resurrection" do not often come from a self-professed atheist to a vicar, so my only possible response was "Of course. See you next week."

After John had gone, I chatted a bit more with Doreen and Caroline, both of whom had decided to stay for lunch. Apparently Frankie had really liked the Lazarus story. We had done it in an all-age service a few years ago, and I had wrapped someone (Jack I think, bribed with the promise of a pizza or t-shirt or something) in toilet roll to play the part of Lazarus, coming out of a "cave" (actually the vestry). Jack, a show-off like his dad, had loved it, first of all coming out like a zombie, only to be told off by me, because the whole point was that he was not a zombie, but a living, normal human being.

"Frankie said, 'Lazarus wasn't a zombie. He was really alive. I want to be like that one day.' He said that to me several times when I went to see him in the nursing home. I had forgotten all about that service till he mentioned it," Doreen explained. "It's funny what stays with you and what goes, isn't it?"

I had completely forgotten about the whole thing until she mentioned it. But it was a good image. Not a zombie, a living person. I want to be like that one day too. Maybe part of my problem was that I was spending far too much time as a zombie in all but name.

These little chats were doing me a power of good. There is something about the freedom to say what you're thinking, to admit what your problems are, that can set you well on the road to a solution. Like any professional, a vicar can put on a mask, pretend everything is fine when it really is not. I had spent over a year wearing a mask that said, "I'm not bothered by death", when in actual fact, I was really worked up about it. Next week would be a real opportunity for me to take that mask off, and I had to be brave enough to take it. □

Pause

In the week between our second and third meetings, my positive mood took a bit of a downward turn. Since the first Monday in Lent, things had been quiet on the funerals front. This was not by choice of course, but simply because no one had rung me up and asked me to take one. I was glad of the breathing space, and, slightly unusually for me, taking advantage of the extra time to get slightly ahead of myself with planning what to do during Holy Week. One of a vicar's challenges is trying to think of interesting and innovative ways of remaining faithful and unchanging. That is to say, you want to give people a new way of thinking about the Easter and Christmas stories, but you do not want to change the content of those stories. Moving between the accounts in each of the Gospels helps with that, but when you think that for some folks in St Mark's this will be the eightieth time they have celebrated Easter, or maybe more, then there are only so many different ways you can say basically the same thing.

I began to think I should probably share some of my own experience over the past few months, weave that into the story of Maundy Thursday, Good Friday, Easter Saturday and Easter Sunday. We never normally made much of Easter Saturday at St Mark's and I was sure that if I did do something, hardly anyone would come. But sometimes the vicar does things for his own benefit as well as for the congregation, and for me, this year, I knew there would have to be something on each of those four days, even if I was alone in the church for one of them. I still had no ideas for Easter Saturday, but that, as it turned out, was just fine.

The more immediate problem came as David, our treasurer, and I, were going through the accounts for the previous year. The church annual meeting was just a fortnight after Easter Sunday, which in practice meant we had to get everything sorted before Easter, because most folks were on holiday the week after Easter. David is a lovely guy, not an accountant or treasurer by trade. He used to be a long distance lorry driver, but get fed up of being away from home so much, so now does deliveries for Argos. He still drives what I would think of as a big wagon, but what he calls "my little truck," and is home every night. He has a good head for numbers and because he now has regular hours, took on the role of treasurer three years ago, when the death of the previous occupant of the role forced a change on us.

David is conscientious, diligent, but not a financial guru, and not a public speaker. So I always present the accounts to the church meeting—that was his one condition in taking the job on. He's happy to talk to folks in the PCC, but not to be the guy at the front. Last year's accounts were fine, and I fiddled on my laptop, producing pie-charts and graphs to show people where their money had gone.

"We had a tight year, last year, Paul." David said, taking a swig of tea. "I'm afraid this year's going to be worse."

"We had a year end surplus of £189. How much worse?"

He just handed me the letter.

For some reason, the wonders at Church House decided they would just tell the treasurers about the financial shortfall that the Diocese had discovered in their accounts. Apparently it meant every church was being asked for an extra five percent in Parish Share.

The idea of the system is that everyone pays what they can afford, with the weaker churches being supported by the richer.

"Ah, this would be why the Bishop's summoned us all to a meeting next week. I did think it was odd, just before Maundy Thursday. I mean two clergy gatherings in a fortnight is a bit excessive."

"Yeah, the manure principle," David smiled. He loved that one. Clergy are like manure. Spread thinly, they do a power of good. Pile them up together and they smell a bit (or perhaps, argue about unnecessary things). Too many leaders and no one to lead, that's the normal problem.

"So what's five percent for us?" A bite of a biscuit, to ease the pain that was coming.

"About two grand. A bit more than our £189 surplus, that's for sure."

"Yeah, and a bit more than we can get through a table top sale. I'm just going to wait and see where the wind's blowing with this one. Maybe the Bishop will have a bit more to say next week. Hand me the letter again."

I was trying to remember the wording.

David raised an eyebrow and then emptied his cup in a gulp, as he waited for me to re-read the letter.

I found what I was looking for: "Parishes are being strongly encouraged to consider an additional contribution. A five percent contribution from every parish would more than cover the predicted shortfall," I read carefully. "Did you spot that—'encouraged to consider an additional contribution,' or in other words 'its not mandatory, because we have not got it through Synod yet, but are asking in the hope of scaring some of you into giving it.' Sneaky bastards."

"You're beginning to sound like my manager," David grinned. "What do you mean?"

"Well, there's no direct order, here is there? Just a plea for help. This is just another begging letter. That's why I didn't know about it. I wonder if this was really the plan for solving the problem. 'More that cover' it said. So if some of us don't pay, then maybe that would be fine. Not a clearly thought out strategy if you ask me. Don't send them anything yet. We'll keep quiet about it until the new PCC after the annual meeting, see how things are turning out then. That okay?"

"Yeah, sure, no problem. If a debt collector comes round, I'll send him your way. Your skinny legs will be much easier to break than mine." He slapped his not inconsiderable thighs and grinned again. A gesture at my empty mug "Fancy another?"

"Yes please. Then let's run through this all one last time. It would be good to get it finished today."

By the time I left David's house an hour later, we were both happy with the presentation of the accounts for the church meeting. I had some pretty pie charts, and a list of number I understood. Progress all round really. We talked a bit more about the begging letter and decided that when I reported the surplus it would make sense for me to point out how small a surplus it was, and that "one unexpected large bill" would have wiped it out. There are often large unexpected bills in church life, normally somehow related to the building, but not always. Someone accidentally leaving the heating on constant for a few days in the middle of winter does damage with the gas bill for example. There are so many ways to bankrupt a church, but I was finding it difficult to come up with ways of helping one grow.

David suggested that maybe this was just how things are nowadays. "Its just that fewer people come to church now. I remember when I was younger, loads of people came, it was just what you did on a Sunday. Now what you do on a Sunday is have a lie in, go shopping, watch telly, all kinds of other stuff. It's nothing personal Paul, they just don't want to come."

David had been part of the PCC discussion, or at least, he'd been in the room, even if he had not really said very much. In his view, the noticeboard was "a bit of a waste of money we haven't got. But it'll keep Tony quiet, so maybe that's money well spent." He was as challenged as

I had been by Richard's gardening suggestion. Richard's seventy-one and thinks it important that he goes out and sorts other people's gardens out, as a way of drawing them closer to Jesus. I had talked with him after the meeting, and we had agreed that we would try and find one or two gardens that needed attention, maybe offering to help some of the folks who come to the lunch club. But that was on the back burner until after Easter, when the weather might be a bit warmer and the vicar might be slightly less busy.

David's suggestion was that we asked the teenagers what they wanted to do. "They're the present, never mind the future. Give them control and see what happens."

A slightly intimidating challenge, but probably one I ought to be taking up. □

Third Meeting

The question had bugged me for most of the week. What passage should we look at in order to answer John's question? I kept settling on a different one each time I thought about it. It was starting to get annoying, so I asked Mary about it on Tuesday night when we were doing the washing up. "I have to pick a passage about the resurrection for the death group. But I can't decide which one. I've got two favourites, Paul in Athens and then Paul talking to the Corinthians about why the resurrection makes sense. What would you pick?"

"Sorry, 'death group'?" Mary paused in scouring a pan and turned to me with raised eyebrows.

"Oh, you know, me and John and Doreen and Caroline. On a Thursday morning. We're talking about death, so everyone has decided to call it the death group."

"Cheerful. But accurate I suppose." She resumed scouring. "Why one passage? Is that a self-imposed limit or what?"

Mary's question answered mine. "My own limit I guess. It's not a conventional Bible study. Neither John nor Caroline seem to want that. So there's no reason why we can't have more than one. We'll have both and see how far we get with either. Thanks love."

"Pleasure. You owe me two kisses for that. Now you can help me decide what topic we need to write letters of complaint about."

I paid my debt full. My first suggestion of ways of disposing of annoying parishioners was dismissed with a flick of soap suds, but the idea of broken electrical goods was approved. Year four were going to write to Currys and complain, and I was now looking forward to Thursday.

We began with Paul in Athens. He is alone, wanders around and sees an altar "to an unknown god" which he uses as a pretext for preaching about Jesus. I personally like the way he uses what is around him and makes contact through what people already know. As I understand it, the Athenians were covering their bases by having this altar, a kind of "this one is for any angry deity we accidentally overlooked, didn't mean to ignore you, sorry, please no smiting" sort of an altar. John thought that was quite amusing. "A bit more than just touching wood or avoiding ladders that is."

Rather than just read the passage and then have a random discussion, I'd decided to read it bit by bit and talk as we went, giving people a chance to disagree, ask questions or say what they were thinking. It seemed to be going okay so far. I explained about how Paul talks about Jesus and the resurrection, and that some people thought he was talking about two gods: a male Jesus and a female *Anastasis*. "Kind of goddess 'Standing upright' or something," I suggested, not quite sure if that was right, but liking the imagery anyway.

"What do you mean?" Caroline was lost.

"Well, the Greek word for resurrection is '*Anastasis*,' and it is hard to be sure, but it seems possible to me that when Paul is talking, some of the people think he is talking about two gods: the god male Jesus and the female goddess '*Anastasis*' or 'standing up' as that is what the word literally means. It's a feminine word, so they would have thought she was a goddess. I think for the Greeks, just as for people today, the idea of someone being dead, passing through death and then coming out the other side walking and talking was a bit odd."

"Well, it is odd," Doreen interjected. "I mean, generally speaking, when people die, they stay dead. All of us are here because we have had someone we love die. So far, they've stayed dead. Personally, I think my Frankie is not going to stay dead forever. But I am quite happy to accept I am in a minority there."

"But how do you know?" John asked. "No offence, but the evidence suggests you're wrong."

"Does it?" she countered. "I think the evidence suggests I'm right."

The perfect opportunity to introduce the second passage. Mary was right (again). I got everyone to flip forward in their Bibles and look at Paul's argument in 1 Corinthians 15. Again, we went for the grand sweep. I talked for about ten minutes, trying to do justice to the big picture of Paul's point.

"So let me see if I've got this right," John asked. "Paul— that's the Paul in the Bible—is saying that if Jesus did not rise from the dead, Christianity is bollocks."

"Maybe not that precise word, but yes," Caroline smiled at him.

"Okay, sorry, Christianity is worthless, a waste of time."

We all smiled at him, encouraging him to continue. "And he says that Jesus' resurrection definitely happened because there are lots of witnesses and that Jesus' resurrection is the first of everyone's, that it is a foretaste, and that when we are resurrected we will be linked to our current selves, but also completely different, like an acorn and an oak tree. He also has no idea when it will happen, but that it will be instant and everywhere when it does. Is that basically it?"

"Yeah, I think so. Thank you John."

"What for?"

"Well, as you know, I have been struggling myself with death and what to think of it all, and hearing you explain it like that has made me realise that if I believe Jesus was raised from the dead, then even though I really do not understand the rest of it, nor do I get the justice of how some people die, it does not really matter, because it is not my problem to understand, simply to trust. So my question to myself is, can I trust God enough to leave the rest to him?"

"That's the big one, isn't it?" Caroline agreed.

"It certainly is," concurred Doreen.

"Don't think I can, if I'm honest," John added. "But it has given me stuff to think about, that's for sure."

We did talk a bit more, but the energy had gone from the discussion, and even though we'd only been going for forty minutes, I suggested we paused there, had another cup of tea and chatted about other stuff. John excused himself: he was part way through PAT testing a small business and wanted to make sure he finished it before the end of the working day. "The bloke didn't complain when I said I was going to church for a meeting with the vicar, but you could see him thinking it was a bit odd. So if I'm back early, all's well really. See ya."

I made the three of us another mug of tea. It may have been close to lunchtime, but all that talking and thinking had made me hungry, so I was glad that there were still a few biscuits left. I munched on one, staring into space.

Caroline coughed. "I thought we were going to chat a bit, not sit in silent meditation?" she gently chided me.

"Sorry. I was just thinking about how difficult it can be to believe sometimes. I mean, I watched my mother slowly decay in front of me. I think it was the fact that her mind went while her body stayed fine for ages. The time lag between the two, if you like. Death is so cruel, it has such a sting, to quote that passage." I gestured at a still open Bible. "But does the sting of death mean we cannot trust in the possibility of resurrection? I think I had started to think that, but since John said what he said, I have begun to wonder if maybe I do believe after all."

"Well Paul, you wouldn't be human if you didn't have doubts sometimes," Doreen suggested. "Over the years I have wondered why God let Frankie be born, live his limited life for so long. I didn't begrudge him the care he needed, don't mind that I never married, although I did wish for kids of my own for ages, but that was not to be. I've gone through that pain and out the other side. So maybe that helps me think of going through death, and out the other side, I don't know."

"There is that line about 'the valley of the shadow of death' after all," Caroline chipped in. "I lived there for months both when Bruce was ill and after he had died. It is normal to have doubts. I wonder if you just haven't made enough space to grieve?"

They were wise people, these two. Maybe that was my problem. I had not made enough space to grieve my parents, nor the funerals I took each month. Maybe that was what I needed. More space to be sad. In the business of life is can be really easy to rush from a funeral to a meeting without stopping to think about the fact that you have just helped a group of people say goodbye to the mortal remains of a human being they loved dearly.

Death sometimes does not seem at all real. It seems like some sort of a trick. It has happened to me a few times. I know someone is ill, have watched and talked with someone as they get older and frailer. Discussed their limitations, watched the world slowly closing in on them. I remember one lady, Rebecca, slowing going blind. When I first met her she was confident, outgoing, full of life. She may have been in her seventies, but could have passed for sixties or even younger. Then her eyesight began to fade. Her once spotless house became shabby. The once sparklingly clean tea-cups became a bit grimy. Her more than daily excursions to the shops or the park or church became a once-a-week shuffle to church on a Sunday morning. When I went to visit her, I started making the drinks, often doing some washing up as well, to ensure we both had a clean cup and she could eat from a clean plate.

I talked with Doreen and Caroline about Rebecca. Doreen had known her far longer than I had. They were good friends. Caroline had never met her, something she said she regretted, "as she sounds a wonderful lady."

"She was. I always knew I could pray with her. Made going to see her worthwhile. She had such faith. We talked a bit about death towards the end of her life. She told me she wasn't afraid, but she was sad. I didn't understand quite what she meant at the time, but I'm starting to think I do now."

It is amazing how conversations come back to you. "Unafraid but sad," is a good motto for facing death. I still have the ache of missing people. I miss Rebecca. I miss my Mum and Dad. I miss Marion. I miss so many great people I have known and loved. Is it okay to miss them and be sort of confusedly unsure about how and when and whether they'll be resurrected, hoping they will, trying to believe it is possible but never completely certain?

Doreen and Caroline said they thought it was and I began to hope that I could think it was too. □

Knock knock

Three pm on a Sunday afternoon. We had celebrating Mothers Day in church and then again at home. I had prepared the food, pizza again, with the promise of something nicer in the evening. But we all needed two hours desk time to get ready for the week. The kids were supposed to be doing their homework. Mary was preparing for the week ahead, which involved both marking and quite a lot of cutting out it seemed. It was cold and miserable outside. I had agreed with Jack and Annabelle that we would have get to work on a gourmet tea at five, if we had all got our work done by then.

As usual I was flipping pebbles out of my inbox. Someone somewhere described email to me like pebbles. Each one is small and not too much bother. But when they pile up, a mound of pebbles is heavy and annoying to deal with. My mound was a bit big so I was sorting them, filing them, getting rid of as many as possible.

I was surprised by how positive I was feeling about Mothers Day. Maybe it was because I had been honest again. I began the service with this "To be honest, I was dreading today. Mother's Day when your Mum is dead is never going to be easy. I know some people hate this service and avoid church because of it. I know other people love it, celebrating their new children, pleased that they have finally been able to have a baby. Whether you love it or hate it, you are welcome here today. I love today because I can celebrate Mary as mother of my two children, and I hate it because my own mother is no longer alive. Maybe you have an equal mix of emotions. Whatever your emotional state, you are welcome here today."

I am beginning to enjoy being honest. It makes life so much more bearable. The service had the usual giving out of flowers to every woman in church, and Sunday school made cards for their own mothers or grandmothers. I talked about Nicodemus coming to see Jesus, about how we may all come in the dark confusion of uncertainty looking to him for light and hope. I had been tempted to talk more about my own thinking about bereavement, but had decided against it. As Mary had put it, "Mothering Sunday is really not the time to talk too much about death Paul. I know you're obsessed, but spare the rest of us."

As I deleted spam emails I ran over the service again in my mind, trying to decide if I had done it well or badly. The jury was still out, with a hint of a possible positive verdict, when there was a knock at the door.

"I'll get it," I shouted. Not that anyone else had moved as far as I could tell. Unbidden, Annabelle's voice echoed in my ear. "I bet its cat lady. Go on, offer her two tins Dad."

Smiling to myself, I went to the door. It was John. "Got a minute?"

"Sure. You want a cuppa?"

"Yeah, please."

We made the tea in the kitchen. Then, equipped with beverages and biscuits, retired to my study. He looked slightly nervous. Glancing around the study, he stuck a finger in his ear, wiggled it, withdrew it and inspected the result. "Sure you've got enough books?"

"Yeah, too many. I've even read some of them. You alright?"

"Fine." He took a sip of tea.

I decided to wait, and just sipped mine, silently, looking expectantly at him. Something was up. John has never been to my house. I may have been in his over fifty times. But he has never been to mine.

"The thing is," John shifted in his chair, "The thing is, I went to church today."

"Go on," I was interested now. Trying not to pounce on him.

John explained. There was no way he would come to St Mark's. Sensibly, he reasoned that if he did, everyone would pounce on him. He would have no chance to just sit and listen, decide what he thought for himself. Also, apparently, if he had thought I was spouting rubbish, he might have heckled. Probably not, but it was possible. Also, he was a bit concerned that maybe I would try and pounce on him as well. Like he was some kind of prize catch from a master angler. But since he did not know the priest at the

Cathedral, and the whole place is pretty big, he decided that he would be fine sitting anonymously in a service.

"That's exactly why loads of people go to the Cathedral John. To sit anonymously. What did you think?"

"Well the music was not to my taste really. And there was a lot of unnecessary poncing about. I mean can't the bloke just walk from one place to another without some other bloke holding a big stick going in front of him? It's not like anyone is going to try and mug him, is it?"

"Fair point," I nodded my agreement.

"And I wasn't really sure what was going on a lot of the time. Fortunately the piece of paper they give you said when you had to stand up and when you had to sit down Why we did, I've no idea to be honest. Its far too long since I've been to church, except for a few funerals, and that don't really count."

Unnecessary ceremony aside, John had been struck by the service, he said. Still not enough to make him stop being an atheist, but enough to make him stop and think. Apparently the talk was quite interesting. The "bloke in a dress, daft idea," had managed to link the Bible story, about some bloke coming to Jesus at night with the fact that many people may want to come secretly to find out more about Jesus.

"It was a bit creepy, to be honest. I hadn't told anyone I was going, but one or two things he said could have been addressed to me. The thing is, me and Marion had got set in our ways, and it was going to be hard for either of us to change. I spent over thirty years telling her I was not going to church with her, and I never felt I could change my mind on that. And it was nice to have a few hours to myself each week, to know I could do errands without worrying, or chill out or whatever. She took the kids with her. I got some peace. Then she went alone, and I still had some peace. Even when she was ill, church was a break for me. I kind of felt guilty about it, but I needed it."

"Everyone needs their own space, nothing to feel guilty about. And I understand what you mean about St Mark's by the way. It would be a hard place for you to walk into. I mean, I would love it if you came, but I really do understand why you might not want to."

"I never even said I'd definitely go back anywhere. Just wanted to come and tell you I'd been once. Felt you ought to know. And that bloke talked about how we cannot just come in the dark, we have to come into the light and be honest about what we're looking for. I thought he had a fair point, and that meant I ought to be honest and tell you I went, and that I may not, or I may, go back. I've enjoyed our group, and I'll come for one more week, but then I think I'm done, if that's okay?"

I had been wondering about the group, what to do, and was grateful for John's honesty. One more week, a chance to wrap things up. I told John I was quite happy with that, and he agreed that I should ring the others and tell them. He finished his tea, thanked me and left.

I watched him walk down the road, pondering what he'd done for me. I remembered the shattered tea cup, the mess of my own life, and his part in putting the pieces back together. Life is funny sometimes, and often not at all what you expect it to be like.

Doreen and Caroline were both happy with the arrangement. "One last chat would be lovely, but things can go on too long sometimes."

We had to end well, of course, and for that I needed the advice of washing up with Mary. ☐

Ending Well

Mary was adamant about communion. "You always say it is the way to bring closure. You even told me to do it for the end of term service, which was a daft idea for a county school with virtually no Christian pupils and hardly any Christian staff. You always say Communion it is the place of healing. Just because John isn't a Christian, why would that stop you? It doesn't stop you on a Sunday, does it?"

Actually, I did not need persuading, I was just playing devil's advocate, to test the strength of the idea. She was quite right. Communion was a fitting ending. I decided to forewarn everyone, and also ask them to do some preparation. I did not want any of them to feel put on the spot, or that they had missed an opportunity.

I kept the details vague on the phone, simply asking them all to come ready to share something they had learned over the past three weeks, and ideally what, if anything, had changed in their thinking about death. I explained that we would have an informal communion service, but we would work out the details once we were all gathered.

"So you going to put on all your gear in here?" John wanted to know as he settled into his sofa, looking slightly naked without a cup of tea in his hand. Caroline and Doreen were, as usual, comfortable on the other sofa. I was in the same chair for the fourth week in a row. Creatures of habit, all of us. "It's not quite the setting for that, is it?"

"Nah. Informal means no dressing up, sorry mate. I'll just say a few words, offer you the bread and the cup, and you decide what you want to do. Short and simple. Somewhere in the midst of it all, I want us to share what we've learnt over the past few weeks."

"You first." John pointed firmly at me. No one disagreed, not even me. No one was in a mood for small talk. That could come later. The serious business might as well begin straight away.

"Okay, I guess I have been learning about how to be human again. I sometimes get too much into role as a vicar, and forget the human cost of death. I don't think I have fully come to terms with my mum's death yet, and this probably is not the place to go into too much detail about that, but I need to find the place where I can, because until I do, I'll just be carrying a festering wound, which hurts me and probably hurts lots of other people as well. I have been impressed by your honesty," I gestured to all three of them, "Thank you for being honest, and for allowing me to hear what you thought, and especially for allowing me to say what I thought and, as far as I know, for that to stay within these four walls."

"Tried to sell the scoop to the Echo, but 'vicar not sure he believes in life after death' wasn't news apparently.' John grinned at me. "Only joking, course I've not told anyone. I am glad to have had a chance to ask honest questions about what it is Christians really believe. I still don't think I believe it, mind you, but at least I've got a clearer idea of exactly why Marion was so hopeful. And it was really good to meet Christians who were less hopeful. Made believing seem possible, somehow."

"I'm glad the vicar did what he was told," Caroline smiled at me. "I needed to talk to someone about Bruce's death, and it has been nice to have an audience of three. Before we finish, I feel that I have to tell you the story of the diamond. It is not so much about the stone as about the chain."

Caroline fished the diamond out of her top and held it up for us all to see. I smiled to myself, remembering the first time I had encountered the diamond. Not something I wanted to repeat, even if there were two other people present.

"Bruce bought me the chain. It was supposed to be my birthday present. I found it in a drawer when I was sorting through his things. I loved the chain, but the glass pendant on it really wasn't me. Didn't like it at all. That was Bruce and jewellery, to be honest. He would get it partly completely right and partly utterly wrong. I've no idea how I would have dealt with it if he had actually been alive to give it to me. But as it was, I had enough spare money from his life insurance to be all silly and get him made into a diamond. I wanted a permanent memorial, but did not want to be constantly going back to Derby to care for a grave or anything like that."

"Sorry, dear, I don't quite follow?" Doreen looked a bit lost, so Caroline explained about how she had had Bruce's remains turned into an industrial diamond and that she was wearing that diamond on a chain that Bruce had bought her. "Oh, I see dear, close to your heart now, isn't he?"

"Yes, that's right."

Neither John nor I could think of anything to say for the moment. I just looked at Caroline, not wanting to make eye contact with anyone else.

"I know some people don't quite understand it, and that's fine. And yes, it was expensive, but I think life insurance is for remembering the dead, so that's what I spent some of it on."

"Makes sense to me. Wouldn't have done it myself, and don't think Marion would have worn me, but I can see why you did it." John offered.

"So can I," I confirmed. "Doreen, what about you, what are you taking away from the past three weeks?"

"Oh, I'm just glad to have had a chance to talk about Frankie. I do miss taking care of him. I sometimes feel lost without having him to take care of. But it was for the best, and although I miss him dreadfully, I am so glad he died before me. I would have hated him to be in a home with no one to care for him."

I had not thought of it that way before, but it made perfect sense. Nursing homes can be horribly anonymous places, and without Doreen's daily visits, I doubt Frankie would have lasted very long in one, and if he did exist in one, it would have been a pale existence, not a thriving life.

"Thank you everyone, for being so honest. Shall we have a brief moment of silence to collect our thoughts and then celebrate communion together?"

We sat companionably for a full two minutes of silence. Communion was very simple: I read a few sentences of Scripture, reminding people of Jesus' words at the Last Supper, bread as body broken, wine as blood poured out, healing for all who chose to take it, whatever their stage of belief. I passed a bread roll around, inviting everyone to take a piece if they wanted. Everyone did, including John. I then passed a silver cup of wine, the small one from my home communion set. Doreen and Caroline drank, but John passed it on.

I prayed for God's blessing on us all: "Father God, you have fed us in this sacrament. By raising your Son Jesus from the dead, you have shown us that death is defeated. Fill us with your Spirit, that we may live your resurrection life, today and always. And the blessing of God Almighty, the Father, the Son and the Holy Spirit be with us now and always. Amen."

The others had all closed their eyes for the blessing, and so only I saw John cross himself, silently, a short movement of his hands from forehead to chest, to shoulder to shoulder. I could not ask him what that meant, because I was not supposed to have seen. Maybe it meant faith, maybe it was habit. Only he and God knew.

"That's all folks," I said hands open gesturing outwards.

"Cheers Bugs Bunny," smiled John. "Can I have a cuppa now? I'm gasping." □

Thursday

"Some of you know that my mum died relatively recently. At least, it feels recently to me. It was in fact well over a year ago, but sometimes the pain of bereavement stays with you for a long time. I have found it difficult to deal with this particular bereavement, far harder to come to terms with than my father's death. It may be because the death of your second parent hurts much more, or it may be the different ways in which they died, the slow decay of dementia for my mother and the relatively swift death from cancer for my father."

Maundy Thursday evening. The usual suspects, all twelve of them, gathered on a gloomy damp night for what I think of as the first instalment of a three-part service. I had decided that I was going to spend some of each of the services talking about part of my own recent reflections on death. It may have just been self-indulgence, but I was going to do it anyway.

"Death is a painfully real reality in our lives. All of us experience bereavement. Some of us experience it when we are quite young, others not until they are older. But eventually all of us will die, and certainly most of us will experience the death of some people who are close to us before we ourselves reach old age.

"How does Jesus prepare his friends for his own death? The first thing he does is to eat with them. From what I have seen and heard when I have spent time with those who know they are dying, close friends and family become more important, and stuff matters far less. People tend to concentrate on close relationships, on making sure that those relationships are in a good place, that what needs to be resolved has been resolved and that forgiveness has been offered and received where that is necessary. Sometimes relationships have broken down to such an extent that forgiveness may not be possible.

"Think of Jesus that Thursday night. He knows he will be dead by Friday afternoon. He knows that the person who will set that chain of events into motion is right here with him in the same room, eating together with him. He knows that the rest of his followers, whatever their brave words, will scatter in fear when the soldiers come, will cower and hide, and that actually it will be the women in his band of followers, women who had no status as legal witnesses, women who were considered as little more than property to be bought and sold, who would be the ones brave enough to go to his grave, and find it empty.

"All of that was for the next few days. At the moment, Jesus is preparing for his own death, preparing to say goodbye, and he does it by calling his closest friends together to eat with him. There is no clear evidence either way—the

Gospels neither affirm or deny it—but I am choosing to think that his mother was with him. I am not so sure about his siblings. They may have been among his followers, or they may have had their own lives away in Galilee or elsewhere. At any rate, those who were close to Jesus were there with him. And he shares himself with them. He tells them more about who he is, how he loves them, how he wants them to live, how they are to spread his message and serve him once he had died. He gives them a means to remember him: bread for a broken body, wine for blood shed to forgive.

"I do not know why God demands death in order for there to be life, but it seems to be written into the universe as God designed it. At least, I think it is. There's a verse in the letter to the Hebrews which talks about how without the shedding of blood there can be no forgiveness. That is simply a background assumption of God's people: disobedience, rebellion against God, the mess human beings tend to make of their own lives is serious, leading to death. Only the death of another in our place is enough to deal with that problem. It may seem barbaric to our ears, but actually we all demand people suffer when they do wrong, we all expect justice to be done, and when it isn't we are outraged. So is it any wonder that God demands justice be done, that there be a death to pay a price that only death can pay? The wonder is that he chooses to pay that price himself, in the person of his Son.

"So there is Jesus, knowing that he was going to die, knowing that everyone had to be ready for his death. The question this asks me today is, am I ready for my own death? Am I ready for the death of those I love? I was ready for my father to die. We prepared well for that, talked things over, reminisced, laughed together, cried together. But my mother's death was so different. Her mind left her long before her body did, and so the goodbye never really happened properly. Maybe if I had prepared myself better while she was fully alive, maybe if she had prepared herself better when she was fully alive, we would have coped so much better. Who knows, it is too late now.

"The only death I can really prepare for is my own. I hope this is not morbid, but I want you to spend a few minutes thinking about your own death. Write your own obituary, or your own eulogy. We'll take about ten minutes for this, which is a long time in a service, I know, but I think it will be worth it. I'll put some music on, pass out paper and pens, and you can use the time as you wish."

They looked slightly blankly at me, as is usual when I do not just follow the liturgy straight through in a fashion some of the regulars have experienced for the past sixty years. But I felt free, and at that precise moment, I needed to feel free. I passed out the paper and pens, put some quiet music on and sat back down. I began to write:

"Paul Harlow was vicar of St Mark's. He did his best for the congregation, but sadly his best efforts were not enough to save the church."

I stopped. Why was I defining myself by my work? At that precise moment I was feeling pessimistic about the future. It is really hard not to when so few people bothered to come out to church on what for me is one of the most important nights of the year. But there has to be more to me than my job, even if I am not very good at it. I had to try again.

"Paul Harlow, husband of Mary, father to Jack and Annabelle. He liked football, but never fully committed to a team. He was a keen cyclist, when he could find the time."

I was struggling. I could write the facts of my early life: where I was born, went to school and so on. I could write a bit abut how I met Mary, even my less than romantic dry-run of a proposal. But who was I really? What did I stand for? What did I live for?

Try again. New piece of paper. I stared at it for a minute or so, willing words to fill the empty void of my life. It had to have some kind of a meaning, some sort of a purpose. Who am I?

I tried these words.

"Paul Harlow, husband to Mary, father to Jack and Annabelle. He did his best to care for other people, but was not always sure if he managed to do that in the right way. He wanted to tell people about Jesus. Sometimes he did, and sometimes he did not. He wanted to be a loving husband and father. Again, sometimes that went well, sometimes he messed up."

I had a rhythm. Who I am is about who I relate to, how I relate to them, how I love, how I care, how I am more than the selfish idiot I often become without really thinking about it.

I wrote for maybe another two minutes, then I stood up, and faded the music into silence.

Some heads were still bowed, some scribbling. Others were looking into space, prayerful or daydreaming, who knew. There was a stillness, reverence space of contemplation. Thirteen bodies physically present, but who knew where their minds were? The present? The past? The future? Regrets, hopes, dreams? Or just hoping the vicar would get on with it, so we could all go home?

"I don't know about you, but I found that really hard. Who am I, what do I stand for, what has my life been all about? These are good questions to ask ourselves at this point in Holy Week. Jesus knew who he was and what he stood for. He knew exactly what his life was about. Can we say that with any degree of certainty? Let us take this uncertainty with us for the next few days, see if we encounter Jesus in and through it."

We moved on in the service, praying together and sharing communion. As I ripped a piece of flat bread into pieces for everyone to eat, I thought of the tearing violence of death, how it comes without mercy, destroying without any qualms. I looked into the cup, full of a deep rich red wine, the colour of oxygenated blood, pumping out of an open wound. Death is so physical. Christianity is so physical. It has to be about more than my head. It must be about my heart, my life, my everything.

I thought of the many endlessly repeating conversations I have with old men and women, whose minds are failing them, who have no real short-term memory any more, who can tell you the same story fifteen times in an hour, each time like it is for the first time. I thought of the bodies wrecked by disease, of cancer eating someone from the inside out.

Of a car crash, and mangled and bloodied limbs cleaned, smoothed and straightened for the family to view. Of the peaceful finality of a corpse laid out for a family to view. Death comes, and we cannot avoid it, we cannot shy away from it. It is horrible, hateful, but it is final and inescapable. Should I run from something I cannot escape?

I always end the Maundy Thursday service in silence, asking folks to pray as long as they like and leave in silence when they are ready. I normally leave last, but today decided to go and wait outside for people as they emerged. One left silently. A few just said goodnight, but most came over to talk to me. No one complained about being asked to contemplate their own deaths. Several said they quite enjoyed the experience. David said it made him think a bit more about what Jesus had experienced.

Charles was appreciative. He had not done what I had asked. "I wrote Ezekiel's eulogy," he told me, waving a folded sheet of paper under my nose. "It was really helpful to have the time and space to do that. I want to go and see the family as soon as I can after Easter. I'm going to look at flights on Friday or Saturday. But now I can prepare the practical bit of going having done the spiritual work. It was good to say goodbye to him, to work out what I could have said, what I will say when we hold a memorial service when I'm there."

Caroline found it a peaceful time. "A chance to think about Bruce, about joining him, about what people might say about me." Doreen said she enjoyed thinking about being with Frankie again. "And the best bit is that he won't have anything wrong with him. I'm really looking forward to that." She smiled, patted my arm. "Paul, you're putting yourself through a lot. I hope you get a rest on Monday, even if you will be busy before then."

I walked home feeling more peaceful than I had in a long while. □

Friday

The next day was a harder service. Good Friday is all about death, and I wanted to stay focused on Jesus' death, not our own mortality. For the Christian, Jesus' death and my death are of a completely different order of magnitude, because the former was volitional and the latter inevitable.

Lots more people come to Good Friday than Maundy Thursday. Maybe it is because its a Bank Holiday, and so they've got the time. Maybe some traditions are stronger than others. At any rate, it is not a service where I felt comfortable being self indulgent for very long, so I kept things short and sweet, although the ending was unexpected, even to me.

"Yesterday evening I talked a bit about my own experiences of bereavement. Some have been easier to cope with than others, which I guess is true for everyone. The death of a distant relative is less painful than the death of a close loved one. Think for a moment about Jesus' mother. She had been visited by an angel, had heard that her son would do great, wonderful, amazing things. Now here she was, in the blazing midday heat, watching the bleeding naked wreck of a man, who had once been a baby in her arms, slowly suffocating as his arms weakened and he was no longer able to bear the agony of raising himself to draw breath on nail-pinned wrists.

"Death is cruel. It is heartless. It does not just destroy the person it takes. It leaves damage and destruction in the lives of all those close by. If you rip up one flower in a closely planted bunch, others may be uprooted or damaged in that one action. Death does this and more.

"The most heartless thing is that none of us knows exactly when we are going to die. Maybe, like my father, you will one day be told that you have about six months to live. That is just a number the doctor makes up. It means 'time is short. Get ready to die.' My dad did, and he was ready to die. Maybe, like my mother, you will slowly realise with increasing horror that your mind is failing you far faster than your body. You do not know when you are going to die, because long before you do die, you stop being you. Maybe you will just go for a lie down and never wake up. Maybe you will be in a car crash. Maybe a lifetime of smoking or eating badly or not taking exercise or having a hard, physical job will take its toll. None of us knows for certain how we will die, but we all know that it will happen some day.

"Part of my job is about death. A significant portion of my work involves helping people come to terms with the death of a loved one. A lesser portion of my work involves helping people get ready to die. I wish I did more of that. I wish we as a nation were better at admitting we are going to die, and getting ourselves ready for it.

"Let us learn from Jesus. He asks for forgiveness for those who have hurt him. They do not know they are crucifying the Son of God, but think they are killing just another criminal. He acts to ensure his closest living relative—his mother—is cared for after his death. He shows mercy to a stranger, offering him hope. He does everything needed to ensure his death is in keeping with God's will. And he experiences abandonment, living without his Father. More than the physical pain of the crucifixion, that spiritual pain is what causes the real agony of the cross.

"Not all of that applies to your or me. Some of it is just about Jesus, about who he is and what he did for each of us. But some of it does teach us. To forgive. To ensure we always do our utmost to provide for our nearest and dearest. To be kind to strangers when we meet them, when we can help them. To live within the boundaries that God sets.

"Most of all, it says to me that I am going to die. And I need to be ready for my own death. Last night I asked people to write their own obituary, or their own funeral eulogy. I did not get very far with mine because I am not really sure what my life is worth or what I have done of any significance. I do my best to love my family, to take care of the responsibilities I believe God has given me and to serve him. I frequently make a complete mess of all of these. But that's okay, because he loves me and helps me sort out the mess.

"So I am left with this question, am I ready to die? I am going to stay in church for a while after the service, thinking about the answer to that question, and spending time in prayer with God. I invite you to stay with me for as long as you want. Tomorrow night, at 11pm, just before Easter Saturday turns to Easter Sunday, I am going to come back to church to talk with God about it some more. This isn't a planned service. There's nothing about it in the notices, but you'd be welcome to join me if you would like to."

Too right there was nothing about it in the notices. I had not planned to say that last thing about Easter Saturday. I had thought we should do something on Easter Saturday, but in the absence of any good ideas I had given up on that plan. In my book, the three-part service is Maundy Thursday night, Good Friday morning and Easter Sunday morning. This extra rogue Saturday night service was not really in my plan of action. I prefer spending eleven pm to one am asleep wherever possible. But I had said it, so I had to do it.

I tried to put it out of my mind as I concentrated on the rest of the service. We had a further time of prayer. I talked a bit about the persecuted church, about how in many countries in the world today, to be a Christian is to risk death. We watched a thirty-minute film of the crucifixion. While I watched it, I was struck again by Mary's agony as I saw her tears at the death of her son. I imagined how I would feel watching Jack nailed naked to a cross, gasping for breath, a slow, agonising death. It made me cry. I think those tears were as much for my mum as for anything or anyone else.

There was quite a lot of death in that service. But then, Good Friday is a day of death. That, to a Christian, is what makes it good. No hope of resurrection or of life just yet. Just misery, agony, god in the rubble of shattered lives and broken dreams.

As the service was drawing to a close, I did remind folks that I was staying to pray, and they would be welcome to join me. I also mentioned that I would be back on Saturday night, but did not do a hard sell. I expected it would be just me, yawning away, but I was wrong. □

Saturday

I managed to stay for over an hour on the Friday. Mainly just sitting, looking at the stained glass Jesus above the main altar in the East Window. Asking myself whether he was interested in my situation, if I had overstepped the boundaries of appropriateness in what I had said. If everything was okay.

I also thought long and hard about whether I was ready to die. My mind went back to John in his kitchen, the shattered tea cup on the floor. My life had felt like that, but now it felt like some of the main pieces were starting to be stuck back together. The cup was still completely unusable, of course, but at least it was recognisably a cup.

Mary thought I had gone a bit mad. She'd been in church for the service, as had the kids, who also thought I was being silly. "You know none of us are joining you Dad, don't you?" was Jack's greeting to me as I sat down to a later than usual lunch.

"Yeah, I know," I said, taking a bite of my tuna sandwich. "To be honest, I will be surprised if anyone joins me. But I've said I'll do it, so I'm going to do it."

Annabelle and Mary confirmed that they would also not be coming. "We'd rather sleep" was the majority view. I kind of agreed with them but was also curious to know if I would be alone, or whether I would have any company at all. As it turned out, three people did join me.

I bet you have already worked out who they were.

Yes, Doreen, Caroline and John. They were all waiting for me when I went over to unlock the church at 10:50.

"Who told you?" I asked John.

"That was me" said Caroline. "I wanted to hear what you had to say tonight, and I thought John might be interested as well. I knew his landline number should be the same as Marion's, since they lived in the same house and all that, so I took a chance."

"And I'm glad she did. Wouldn't normally come to church at this hour—or ever, if I'm honest, but I am a bit curious about what you've got to say." John confirmed.

I let them in and we agreed to wait until ten past eleven before we started. "That's enough time to put the kettle on" said Doreen, and busied herself in the kitchen. She was far more capable than Joan thought, but that was a conversation for another time. Caroline followed her. I looked at John. "You sure you want to be here?"

"Yes. Wouldn't miss it for the world."

By ten past there was no sign of anyone else, so I led them to our usual room. "I missed the services Paul, so tell me what this is all about, will you?" John wanted to know.

I explained about what I had said on Thursday and Friday, stressing in particular the importance of contemplating your own death. "I can't actually remember word for word. And I am not entirely sure where the comments about Saturday night came from. I just found myself saying it, and the thing is, once I'd said it, there was no real way I could retract it. I expected to be here on my own for maybe twenty minutes and then creep off to bed."

"Well if nothing else, I'm staying for the hour to make sure you do your job," grinned John, slurping his tea.

"I think there's something powerful about a vigil of some kind, you know, darkness to light, death to life, all of that," said Caroline. "Maybe we could finish our drinks and then just have a short service from ten to midnight to ten past?"

"So long as its a make it up as we go along service, sure." I agreed. "But while we wait, John, can I tell you something. Do you remember the first time I came to see you after Marion died?"

"Yes, broke her cup, didn't I. Still got it in a box. Don't know why, don't think it could be fixed."

"I bet it could be. As I was sitting in church yesterday, I realised that I felt a bit like that cup. You know, dropped, shattered, broken. Now I feel like someone has started to mend me. Lots still to do, only the main pieces are in place so far. But there's hope, of a sort."

Doreen smiled. "I think I know what that feels like. Shattered but not destroyed, is that it?"

"I guess so."

"Oh, me too," agreed Caroline.

"Still in pieces, me" said John. "But there's the possibility of healing."

We talked about what it felt like to be shattered. Caroline shared something about repairing broken cups, something that gave me an idea for Easter Sunday morning. Even broken things can be beautiful if you know what to do. The conversation turned to how we might remember our brokenness before God. We agreed what to do and shortly before midnight, we all went into the main sanctuary of the church and stood round the communion table, which is on a slightly raised dais about thirty feet closer to the congregation than the high altar. I lit four candles, and then went to the main light switches, and turned them all out. I stumbled my way back to the others, nearly tripping over a chair in the process.

"Careful, now's not the time to break a leg." John's amusement was clear from the tone of his voice, even though I could hardly see his face.

"Oh, I don't know. I fancy the morning off."

We stood, each in front of one candle, faces barely illuminated as they flickered. As my eyes got used to the lack of light I began to see more, feel more comfortable in the gloom. Time to face the dark.

"Jesus died, and descended to the dead. The prince of light was snuffed out and the world was in darkness."

We all extinguished our candles, John nipping his with forefinger and thumb, the rest of us blowing ours out.

"We stand in the darkness. Our lives feel like they are in darkness. Death has ended precious relationships, left us hurting, in pain, unsure and uncertain of the future. We wait in the dark for a new light to dawn."

And so we waited. We may have rushed the first bit. I have genuinely no idea of exactly how long the wait was. Probably about four minutes, maybe more or less. It was peaceful. After a while I realised that it was not actually all that dark. That I could see the others' faces, shapes of furniture, the cross on the high altar. Even when we think we are in the dark, there is usually some light.

On the stroke of midnight, my phone began to play the Hallelujah chorus. I let it play and then said, "Christ the light of the world is risen. Let us live in his light."

I relit my candle and the others lit theirs from mine. We had placed some others near by, and lit those as well, until there were about thirty candles lit on the table in front of us.

"In his light we say that death is defeated. Death no longer controls us. The shattered pieces can be made whole again."

We stood for a while in the candlelight, each lost in their own thoughts, staring at the candle flames, not really noticing the others were there.

155

Then we all looked up at once and smiled.

"Happy Easter folks. Shall we head for home?"

Doreen yawned. "Yes, not long before we're back here."

Caroline had promised her a lift home, so they headed for the exit together. John said he'd be fine walking. I turned on a few lights, then went back to blow out the candles. Caroline and Doreen had already gone, but John stayed, "Don't think you should be in here alone at this time of night, you never know what might happen."

I was touched by his concern. As we left he said, "My cup's still shattered. I will work on putting it together, but it will be a long road. Thanks for setting me on the journey."

"Absolute pleasure mate. Stay in touch."

"Sure. Come round for a cuppa whenever you fancy one, but no God talk."

"I'll take you up on that offer sometime."

We went our separate ways. □

Sunday

"Why are you supergluing a cup together at 7:45am on Easter Sunday morning?"

It was a fair question from Annabelle, but I had one in return, "How come you're up so early in the holidays?"

"Chocolate for breakfast, of course. Its Easter Sunday, Mum always lets us."

That was a good response, but I refused to explain myself, telling her she would have to wait for the sermon, like everyone else. This was probably the wrong answer, but I did not really want to have to explain this any more times than I had to.

I love the Easter Sunday service. The songs are great, everyone is always happy, there are normally more people in church than usual. The next day is an extra free day off.

I was both looking forward to, and dreading, the sermon, but I had to follow through one what I had said the night before.

"Those of you who came on Good Friday heard me mention that I was coming here at eleven pm last night to pray. A few folks did join me, and I shared something with them that I also want to share with you.

"For a little while now, my life has felt a bit like a broken cup. Like it was shattered in pieces. Maybe you've had one of those accidents where a teacup hits a tiled floor and the teacup shatters. Sometimes normal life can feel a bit like that. Mine certainly did.

"But the thing is, you can glue a broken cup together." I got my inexpert effort out, to prove the point.

"I dropped this cup this morning. And I glued it back together again today. It is not an expert job, and you can clearly see that, can't you? But my point is this, broken things can be fixed, messes can be mended, shattered does not have to be permanent.

"We follow a God who is in the business of taking our mess and sorting it out. He even did that with death, the biggest mess any of us face. I still have all sorts of problems and questions and doubts. But I am starting to believe that maybe he is the one who can make things a bit better, take the broken pieces and start to make them whole.

"Last night someone told me that the Japanese have an art called *kintsugi*. Skilled craftsmen, far better at this than my poor effort, repair shattered pottery. But they do not just use glue, they use lacquer mixed with powdered gold to repair the cracks. The shattered cup becomes even more beautiful than the original. The cracks remain, but now they shine with gold. There is no attempt to hide the breakage.

Instead it becomes part of something more beautiful. Last night I began to think that maybe God can do that with my life as well. The scars remain, but now they shine, as it were."

I did talk some more about the message of Easter Sunday, Jesus passing through death and out the other side, holding out his hand in an open invitation, asking us to join him. The normal sort of things you might expect a vicar to say on Easter Sunday morning.

I had scanned the congregation at the start, spotted both Doreen and Caroline, but there was no sign of John. I know he was not there, because we had communion, and I gave bread or a blessing to everyone there. He was not one of them.

On the way out, Charles spoke to me, "Thanks for that comment at the start of your sermon, Paul. I have been struggling to work out what to make of Ezekiel's death. I got somewhere on Thursday night, and now I've got a bit further. I've booked flights to go out. Got a decent last-minute deal. It's via Amsterdam, there's a bit of a wait, but I'm happy to pay in time, not pounds. I'm going tomorrow, for three weeks. Denise is going to take care of the cafe while I'm away."

"Safe travels Charles. Let me know when you're back and we can talk some more. I really want to know how it all works out and how you're feeling."

I really did. I knew it would be a tough conversation, that I would be reminded of how privileged I am, a member of the richest two-percent in the world and all that. I wanted to remember how precarious life is in most of the world, how blessed I am to be alive with healthy children and a healthy wife. I needed to be reminded of the whole breadth of God's world, its challenges and opportunities, joys and sorrows.

Doreen gave me an Easter card. "I've given Jack and Annabelle chocolate eggs. I thought you could probably cope without one."

I patted my midriff. "My stomach thanks you."

Caroline gave me a peck on the cheek. "Well done vicar," she smiled. "You seem a bit lighter somehow, like you've left something heavy somewhere. Don't go find it and pick it up now, will you."

Mary had heard this last bit. "Yes, he does have a habit of sometimes carrying the world on his shoulders. But I think this bit was his own to put down, and hopefully leave down. No need to carry it any more. Just so long as he doesn't go round breaking any more of our cups as sermon illustrations. I'm going home, to put the roast on. See you in a bit." Another peck on the other cheek.

Caroline smiled. "I left Bruce at home today. Decided I didn't need to wear him everyday. It was starting to feel a bit morbid. I'm glad I did it, but maybe he'll be just fine at home for a while."

Late that afternoon, after more roast lamb and roast potatoes than a heart specialist could honestly recommend, I needed a stroll. No one wanted to join me, so I decided to walk down to John's house.

He was in. "Hi Paul, just got back. Come in."

I was curious. Had he been to the Cathedral again? Was he on the way to becoming a Christian? Should I ask? Was that too much pressure? He interrupted my silent quandary.

"Yeah," he continued. "Went to do a spot of fishing. Haven't been for ages, what with Marion being ill and all that, sitting on a river bank for hours was not really on the agenda. But I've got the time now, and it was quiet and peaceful. I could look at the water, think about life, no one telling me when to sit down or stand up or sing or anything like that. You fancy a cuppa?"

"Go on, just a quick drink. I'm supposed to be going for an afternoon walk to work off lunch."

"Alright then, once round the park first, then." He reached for his jacket. "Come on, no dawdling."

Off we went. We did not talk much as we walked, just enjoyed the hint of spring that was in the air, the beginnings of real heat in the sun, the daffodils swaying in the breeze.

"Supposed to rain tomorrow. But it is a Bank Holiday Monday, so what do you expect." John smiled. "Think I'll have a sort out, get rid of all Marion's old clothes and that. Or at least get it all bagged up, ready to take to a charity shop. What're you going to do?"

"Dunno really. See what the kids want to do. Possibly shopping or the cinema if the weather's bad."

"Life goes on then."

It certainly does.

The Preacher's Mail-Order Bride

Mail-Order Brides of Sweet, Texas, Book Two

Mail-Order Brides of Sweet, Texas, historically inspired clean and wholesome romance.

Hold onto your bonnets you're about to meet the biggest matchmaking cupid of the west…

Mail Order Bride Gabby Anson is not who she seems. But, getting shot on the stage, having her belongings stolen and then finding out her groom isn't expecting her is more than she's bargained for when she struck out for Texas.

Now the question both she and the surprised preacher, Jarred Andrews want to know is who sent for her and where do they go from here?

Jarred's waiting on the bride the Lord's going to send him when the time is right. But what is he supposed to do with Gabby?

There's a mystery in the tiny town of Sweet when mail-order brides begin to show up for the men one at a time and the town wonders who sent for them. The brides and the grooms wonder more.

Watching them work out the situation is the fun part.

At least it is for Big John Wiggins a widower who knows the joys of a happy marriage and the six foot, five inch widower has decided the men of his town need wives and joy too. Even if it takes him to bring the women to them.